AF278739

in wake of
water

sbr martin

The Artists' Orchard, LLC

This book is a work of fiction. Any references to historical events, real people, or real locales are used fictitiously. Other names, characters, places, and incidents are the product of the author's imagination, and any resemblance to actual events or locales or persons, living or dead, is entirely coincidental.

The quotes in Chapter 8 that tell the story of Creation were taken from the public domain King James Version of the Bible found at www.biblegateway.com.

Copyright © 2011 Sarah Beth Martin

Edited by Sherry Linger Kaier

Cover Photography and Author Photo by PicChick Photography by Lizzy Bittner

All rights reserved. No part of this publication may be reproduced or transmitted in any form or by any means, electronic or mechanical, including photocopying, recording or any information storage and retrieval system, without permission in writing from the publisher except in the case of brief quotations embodied in critical articles or reviews. For information, please address:

The Artists' Orchard, LLC
P.O. Box 113317
Pittsburgh, PA 15241
www.theartistsorchard.com

ISBN 13: 978-0-9843166-8-7
ISBN 10: 0-9843166-8-X

Library of Congress Control Number: 2011912307

Produced and Printed in the United States of America

They say that when one door shuts, another opens.
Thanks to those who were waiting on the other side.

in wake of
water

~ 0 ~

"Help me die, Tad. Please, help me die."

At some other point in time, spoken by some other character, these words might have meant something entirely different. They might have been a plea for mercy or a cry for relief. They might have been a joke or euphemism for something else. They might have made sense.

But here, now, from her lips, they weren't, and they didn't.

She was 26 years old. She wasn't ill, hungry, beaten, or raped. She was just in a place she did not want to be.

"I have to die, Tad. I'm not supposed to be here. Can't you see that? They all left me. They're waiting for me. I have to be with them again… And, there's only one way."

Fifteen years ago, her mother died. One year later, her older sister, her only sibling, died. Another year later, her father died. Such was the end of her immediate family, the explosion of her nuclear unit.

As the sole survivor of this localized Chernobyl, at 13 years old, she moved in with her Aunt Margo and Uncle David. From that time on, Margo and David provided her with unlimited financial support and made sure that all of her physical needs were met. Yet, they couldn't give her what she truly needed, the one thing to which she'd grown most accustomed.

In all the years she lived there, neither Margo nor David had ever regularly delivered to her any physical or vocal expression of love. Life with them was without hugs, kisses, and smiles. It was without a sense of belonging.

Margo and David were cold, linear people. They treated

her like an obligation rather than a person. Their spasmodic conversations with her were vacant and superficial, their sentences articulated with perfect pronunciation, direct diction, and systematic syntax. Each syllable spanned out across measures of deliberate hesitation.

To them, life was procedural and calculated. Everything could be reduced to mathematical terms which fed into precise formulas that equated to predictable outcomes. It was all about control. *They needed it. They wanted it. They could not go without it.*

They carefully crafted every aspect of their lives. They'd tried, too, to carefully craft her life, to impose logical quadrants, into which discrete functions could be graphed, over her being. This they saw as their duty—a duty to fashion her parameters, to define for her some fixed set of vertical and horizontal outer bounds. In so trying, they overlooked her most vital dimension—her depth. Indeed, her depth had no place in their design.

Her life with Margo and David was in diametric opposition to what she enjoyed when her immediate family walked the earth. Years ago, she joked, laughed, and loved. She had fun. Her family was a tight unit of four, bound physically by warm embraces and soulfully by warm emotions. Life with them was full. It had meaning.

She had been one in a set of four. But now, three of the four were gone, missing, somewhere else, and she felt out of place with Margo and David.

She'd lost something, maybe everything, as her family, one-by-one, left this world. She kept looking for that something and, when she couldn't find it, she concluded that it wasn't on this earth. They must have taken it with them when they left. And now she knew where it was and what she had to do to get it.

She'd reasoned it out over and over again in her head.

Each time, she came to the same conclusion: she had to die. She had to die to be with her family. That was the only way she could get back whatever it was she'd lost. But she didn't want to wait. She wanted it now. For her, the ends were grand, and certain, enough to justify the severity of the means.

"Will you help me, Tad?"

What? Why is she asking me this? What does she want me to do? I can't do anything. I can't help her. I want no part of this. I will not help her die!

"Help me die, please." Her voice reached him, even though he was anxious with thought. He focused his gaze on her face and followed the salty black lines on her cheeks up to the puddles of tears pooling her eyes.

Eyes, windows to the soul. I saw a movie once where a priest put pennies over a dead woman's eyes. I wonder if they'd do that to her, put pennies on her eyes? She has big eyes. Too big for pennies. Maybe nickels. No, quarters. She has eyes like quarters. Big eyes, covered with quarters, closed forever.

"Die?" he asked.

No matter how hard he tried, Tad could never really speak more than a few words at a time. What words he did utter were usually repetitions of those he'd just heard or standard replies and catchphrases. He wasn't slow or disabled. He had no problem hearing or reading words—he just had trouble speaking them aloud.

He was dull on the outside, but, deep inside him, he had words and sentences that mattered. Rapid fires of words and ideas continually shot off in his head. Wracking sentences collided and intersected. New words and notions impregnated formulated deliberations, making them bulge and burst into the reverberating, murmured pulse of convoluted thoughts and emotions which he could not translate into spoken words.

He breathed his words rather than speaking them. Every time he opened his mouth to speak, he would exhale and his words were reduced to molecules of air which tumbled out of his mouth without taking the time to aggregate into an audible phonetic tone. They scrambled into the air around his face, the air he breathed. As he inhaled, he would suck those words back into his mouth. From his mouth they circulated through his entire body before reaching his mind again. Once again in his mind, those words rode the rhythms of his cognition; some surfed the peaks while others embedded themselves in the pits.

He'd been this way for over a decade, since around the time his father died. He just woke up one morning and couldn't speak the way he used to. The words wouldn't come out right, despite his efforts. He would stutter and twitch each time he tried to speak his mind. Soon enough, he stopped trying and acquiesced to his weakness.

Most everyone attributed Tad's condition to his father's death. They reasoned that the trauma was too much for Tad to bear, that it made him turn inward and seek shelter within himself.

Tad was the one who'd found his father's body. It was an otherwise ordinary day. He came home from school, threw his book bag on the sofa, and ran upstairs to change out of his school clothes. He heard the shower running. He expected that his mother was still at work and assumed it was his father bathing.

After changing, he ran back downstairs to get a snack. As he rounded the corner from the dining room to the kitchen, he slipped and fell on what he soon discovered was a patch of vomit and feces expelled from his father in the final moments of his life.

Tad hit the floor. His bare legs, arms, hands, and face

were spackled with this mess. He screamed in disgust. Then he saw him—his father—lying there, naked and wet, face-down on the floor, his right arm extended outward, pointing toward the end of the kitchen counter, some three feet away, where the phone was. *Dead.* Tad crawled through the gruesome muck and touched his father. He was cold, wet. *Dead.* He shook his father. He called out his name. *Dead.*

Tad didn't know what to do. He was scared and confused. His mother would be home soon. She'd know what to do. He lied down on the floor and buried his head in his father's shoulder. Cuddling his father's corpse and gulping the stench of stale shit and puke as it crusted on his body, he was motionless on the floor for over an hour before his mother got home.

"Yes, die. I want to die. And, I want you to help me. I'm going to die whether you help me or not, but I'd really like it if you helped. It would mean a lot to me."

It would mean a lot to her? What about me? What about what I want? I want her to live. But I guess that doesn't matter. I guess I don't matter either. I must not mean a lot to her. If I did, she wouldn't want to die. She'd want to stay here with me.

No, she doesn't want that. She wants to die to be with them. God, what a risk! She's willing to give up the certainty of her life for an afterlife that might not even exist. Why would she want to do that?

He'd been staring down at his hands, trying to let the words out of his mouth. There was so much he wanted to say. Head raised, he looked at her and then looked away, staring at the space beside her, "Help you?"

They'd been friends for about three years now, but known each other for over ten. Tad was 21 years old. She used to sit for him when he was younger, when he was 10 and she was 15. Back then they weren't friends though. And they certainly weren't friends for the eight years that followed.

Eight years, however, allowed them to grow so apart that they could come together again in a new way. They met up one day and spent every day after that together. It was a silent, abrupt induction into an outwardly illogical relationship.

They weren't lovers or anything like that, at least not in any physical sense. They were just two friends who'd found something that transcended give-and-take. Neither had to do anything to accommodate the other; both were free to just be.

Though they were amazingly different people, their differences complimented each other, making each fuller than either was before. She didn't mind his sparse communication. If anything, she reveled in it. He was there to listen to her, to absorb the words and sentiments that deflected off of many others with whom she attempted to communicate.

Melodramatic, histrionic at times, she spoke rapidly, with an uncanny expressive fluidity. She was entertaining, honest, and unrestrained. Most importantly, she spoke to Tad even though most others didn't. Those others thought Tad wasn't worth the time or the effort. They thought he was broken and empty. Hollow. Retarded. Not her though—she fed him a steady supply of conversation. Her words continuously regenerated in the air he breathed. He swallowed them along with his own, allowing them to cross-breed in his mind. He liked her words. They belonged to him.

"Okay, listen, Tad. Let me tell you something."

"Okay."

"Sometimes, I'll be out. I'll be out in like a restaurant or a diner or something. And, I'll be sitting there at a table eating my food and I'll stare at my glass. Water, beer, soda, whatever. I'll stare at it. And, I'll think. Do you know what I think, Tad?"

No response.

"I stare and I think—no, I fantasize—about picking up that glass and pouring it out over my head, letting it drench me, soak me from head to toe. I don't care if people would stare at me, or what they would think… I've wanted to do that for so long, Tad. I think about it all the time."

He pictured her doing this. He wanted to smile and laugh. But he couldn't. Instead, he was moved, moved by the image of her so raw and so free. Her hair was long and wavy, like the hair-shroud of a young Venus. *Boticelli.* He imagined liquid dripping from its length. He saw her towering above him with this wet hair, and him, drinking the swollen drops that would drip slowly to his mouth. *Oh, to taste her water!* For him, this image was beautiful—pure and reassuring. *Like a kitten sucking at its mother's tit.*

"And, whenever I made up my mind, when I decided that I have to die, I just kept thinking about it more and more. I couldn't stop—I couldn't get the idea out of my mind. And, I figured that must really mean something. That must mean that I have to do it before I die. I have to. And, then I started wondering why. Why would I have to do something like that? Then, it hit me! I realized that I have to do to it so that I don't go to hell.

"See, Tad, I can't go to hell. I would hate it there. I know I would. They aren't there. They can't be. They have to be in heaven. If I went to hell, I wouldn't be with them. I'd be all alone… I can't go to hell, Tad! That's why I have to do this before I die. That's why I can't stop thinking about it—it's like my heart is telling me that I just have to do it or I'll go to hell.

"Now, I'm sure you're wondering what this has to has to do with going to hell. I asked myself that question too, Tad. I thought about it for a long while. And, then I found an answer—one that makes perfect sense."

Sense? None of this could ever make perfect sense. Any answer she'd find is to a question she should have never asked. Sense. What is sense? Is it this? Is it her? It can't be. Sense went away when she started thinking like this.

"I'm ready to die. I'm ready to be with them again. So, I have to get to heaven because that's where they are. But, I've done, well, you know, a lot of bad stuff in my life. And, maybe some of it was so bad that God wouldn't let me in to heaven. It's like I have all these sins, and if it wasn't for my sins I could get in to heaven. That's when I figured it out. I need to get rid of my sins. I need to clean myself so that God'll let me in.

"I know you're Presbyterian and all—and I don't know much about that religion. But, I'm Catholic. Or, I was Catholic. And, Catholics baptize little babies. They pour water over the baby's head to wash away its sins. Sure, they're babies and couldn't have sinned much in their little lives, but there's some thing called original sin, and that's what they wash off of the babies. But, they can baptize adults too, Tad. Like an adult who converted from another religion or something. And, when they baptize an adult, they wash away all of his sins, the original sin and the actual sins he committed.

"They say that when a person is baptized and all his sins are washed away, God instantly forgives him for everything. God won't punish him for what he did before he was baptized. And, if he dies before he commits another sin he automatically goes to heaven.

"That's exactly what I want, Tad! I want to automatically go to heaven when I die. And, that's got to be why I couldn't stop thinking about pouring a glass of water over my head. I need to have all my sins washed away. I need to be baptized.

"I'm not talking about being baptized in a church or anything. Even though I was raised Catholic, I'm not Catholic anymore. I believe in God and stuff. I just don't buy into organized religion. And, I know that baptism is part of orga-nized religion. But, I want the part of it that's not.

"It's nothing but process in the Catholic religion. It's something Catholics do because they're told they have to. When they baptize little babies, the babies don't know what's happening—they're not making a choice. But, I'm old enough to know what's happening, Tad. I'm old enough to make a choice."

She's old enough to make a choice. But she can't see fault in the choices she's made. She's decided to end her life. She's decided to die. Her God gave her free will, and look what she's done with it.

"I want God to forgive me and let me go to heaven. I don't care what God it is—if it's the Catholic one or one from some other religion. I just want him to know that I have faith in him, that I'm sorry for everything bad I've ever done and want his forgiveness.

"You know, Tad, it's what baptism represents that's im-portant. It's a symbol of God's forgiveness and acceptance. And, anyone who wants that forgiveness and acceptance should be able to get it no matter what religion they are, if they're even any religion at all.

"I'm sure that there are plenty of ways to seek God's forgiveness before you die. I'd bet every religion has its own special way. But, I'm not too interested in what any organized religion would say. I'm just interested in what my heart's been telling me. It's been telling me to wash my sins away… Catholic ideas about baptism may help to explain what I'm seeking—but, it's just chance that there's a term for what I have to do."

She'd been baptized, officially and for real according to the Catholic Church, 26 years ago, shortly after her birth. Her immediate family was Catholic, but not retentively so. Though they regularly went to church on Sundays and observed denominational holidays, they weren't steadfast to all of the procedural edicts of Catholicism. Rather, her parents tried to instill in her the fundamental precepts common to most organized religions—a respect for life, one's dignity, and one's soul and culpability for one's own actions.

Margo and David were Presbyterian. When she moved in with them after her family passed, they afforded her freedom of religion. She was told she could remain Catholic and bear out her religion in the sacrament of Confirmation, or, if she so desired, she could convert to Presbyterianism. She opted for both though she chose neither. In fact, she formulated her own religion, one where she needed only to adhere to those fundamental precepts her parents had taught her and to simply believe that there was a God who had made and loved her.

As she got older, and reflected on all that had happened in her life, she questioned whether that God had abandoned her. But she never doubted that he had, at some point, been there and made her. She never doubted that he existed. And if God was out there, she was certain she could reach him.

"That's where you come in, Tad. That's how you can help me… The more I thought about it, the more I realized that I shouldn't be the one to baptize myself. Someone else should do it. I couldn't ask Father Paul—he baptized me when I was a baby, and it'd be too weird to ask him to do it again. Plus, I really don't want him to do it. Like I said, I'm not looking for religion. I just want to be clean, to get forgiveness…

"I'd like you to baptize me, Tad. I want you to do it."

Me, baptize her? Can I, could I, do that? She's not asking me to pull a trigger. She's not asking me to kick a stool out from under her. All she wants is for me to pour water over her head. Is it water she wants? Why not soda, why not beer?

Fizzing bubbles of sin rolling over her scalp and face,

maybe the carbonation would be too violent and stir too many memories. Sticky lines of syrup, frothy trails of hops, maybe the sugar and preservatives would be too dirty and leave too much behind.

Soda or beer would not do the trick. Neither would wash her sins away. They'd only wake her sins to coat her. The carbon would remind her; the carbohydrates would bind to her. She'd still have her sins, stuck to her. She'd carry them with her. She would not be clean.

No, it must be water. It's water she wants, she needs. Only the stillness and pureness of water could wash her sins away. Only water could make her clean.

Am I to pour this water? If that's all she wants, should I do it? She's going to kill herself anyway. I can't stop that. This is how she wants me to help her. How ever ridiculous her reasoning, could I deny her this simple request?

Tad felt light-headed from the heavy thoughts he could not avoid thinking. She'd lit a cigarette at some point during her diatribe, though, when exactly, he hadn't noticed. Tad watched the smoke billow from the cigarette's tip. It seemed that each spurt of smoke followed the same graceful pattern. He was amazed by its uniformity. The jets of smoke flew onward and upward so swiftly in the air. He felt as light as the smoke, yet blighted that he could not resist gravity.

"I really think you're the best person to do it. For a lot of reasons. I figure you'd like to know, after I was gone, that you helped me find heaven. And, if you were the one to wash my sins away and make sure that all was forgiven, then… maybe… I don't know… maybe that would mean that you, like… that you completely forgave me too. And, that… that's something I want. I want you to forgive me for what we did."

Forgive her? For what "we" did? I didn't do anything. What is she talking about?

Tad didn't want to ask her any questions. He didn't want to hear any more of her absurd answers. They endured a moment of silence as she smoked what was left of her cigarette.

She snuffed the butt in the ashtray. The charming ballet of smoke ended in concert with the closing of a chapter of tonight's conversation, "So, that's it, Tad. That's what I need you for. I need you to baptize me… And, save me from hell."

~ 1 ~

Theirs was a town of southern drawl—both in tongue
and ear and in practice and livelihood. Life seemed to move
in slow motion, the cusps of long workdays fading into long
leisurely nights. Perhaps life moved at this slowly warped
speed because the air was so thick: each breath somewhat
strained, all ambulation and dexterity compromised as if
every motion was set in the undertow of a deep pool of water
with raging rapids above.

With this slow movement came slow work and slow,
slurred thought—all things governed by the dogma of drawl.
There was a cyclic slowness to it all. Slowness begat slowness begat slowness, ad nauseam. This cycle had become the
norm. Rest assured, things got done in this town, albeit at
reluctant pace.

It was a conservative, pro status quo, town. No one
ever really noticed the drawl of life there, but they strived
to maintain it nonetheless. Those few that did notice and
challenge the awry rhythm of life—those that tried to run
at quick-time double-speed between the dense molecules
of air—were seen as "raging liberals" and were quickly
shunned by the town's collective voice and beaten down by
the town's unified down-bowing brow. This disapproval was
often enough to subdue a liberal's rage. For most everyone
knew that, sure enough, the town always got its way—open
minds would be shut, loud voices silenced, by any means.

A liberal who would not, or could not, cease always
ended up, by some stage-managed means, dropping a plastic
baggie filled with an ounce of reefer a few feet away from
a law enforcement officer or having a suspicious box, later
found to contain illicit photographs of young children,

mailed and tracked to his home.

Thus, for the "raging liberal" who wouldn't shut his mind or mouth there remained only two options: (1) stay here, in this town, locked up in jail or the sanitarium, labeled depraved, or (2) leave this town and go somewhere else. Most chose the latter.

Those that chose to leave didn't leave much behind. It was a backward town, divided by prejudices and narrow minds into several distinct social strata, each coated and glossed with antediluvian social mores and norms that operated to prevent the cultural erosion and friction that had worn down such classifications elsewhere in the world. It was inexorable, implanted in the town's shared mentality and implemented ostensibly by its maladapted zoning regime.

From an abstract topographical view, the town was a large circle containing a finite set of squares apiece consisting of a finite set of lines—each line throbbing and pushing another, each square moving in constricting rotation to avoid merging with the next. These lines and squares, set in motion within the motionless circle, were what kept time in this town. It was a broken cog, weighed down by the slothful perpetual motion of the gears cloaked within, laboring the second hand of an invisible clock that kept time fifteen minutes behind the rest of the world.

The geographic, and visceral, center of town was, more or less, a concrete island recessed from the town's automotive thoroughfares and set apart from its residential quarters. This island, cleverly coined the "Atrium," sat isolated and detached from the rest of the town on a raised square of smooth cement freckled with red brick-inlayed sauntering paths exemplifying its restriction to pedestrian pass-through alone.

Although no car or inanimate vehicle of any kind ever traveled the spread of the Atrium, there was usually a human queue trafficking its paths on any and every given business day. Those that traversed the Atrium's trails did so with down-cast heads, possibly to be efficient and get on with their business with little or no human interface or, perchance, to ensure that their gaits were confined to the fixed, prosaic pedestrian routes.

This all made for an interesting aural experience. Devoid of any vehicular purr, of any bellow of rubber on asphalt or steel on steel, one could hear only the shuffling of feet interjected, on minute occasion, by fortuitous salutations, hollow conversations, and jarring coughs, sneezes, and grunts.

Each of these things, and little more, seemed to echo throughout the Atrium, creating a cacophony of muffled remnants of human noise that lingered on far after the cessation of the interpersonal or biological performances that had generated the din and flouted the looming hush which encapsulated the Atrium.

The echoes reflected and refracted off of the buildings in the Atrium before eventually being sopped up by the polyester garb of co-walkers as they footed alongside each other in scattered clusters of like kind. Silence would, again, prevail until the next haphazard human clicks and coughs disrupted the equilibrium in the air, rebirthing the same familiar vacillation. Undeniably, quietude after quietude was successively quashed but not forgotten.

As it happens, silence was a virtue, a prize, for those that frequently beat the brick paths. They hungered for it—it, a form of solace, an acoustic reverie for and from the hard-workers and fast-talkers of this town; it, a chance to stride with the elite masses in cultivated pseudo civility, to dodge social obligation and identification in pursuit of anonymous diplomacy.

For those with such an appetite, the Atrium eagerly provided ample sustenance, habitually gorging its walkers with the raw victuals they craved. A prime example of everlasting closed-circuitry, the walkers fed off of the quiet stillness they perpetuated.

This stillness, coupled with the hard, grey structural topography of the paths and buildings, rendered the Atrium a somber place with its own bland, overbearing personality. The Atrium, an unfriendly and uninviting host, with its personality, and by its design, demanded acclimation, assimilation, and allegiance from its guests, offering only shallow consolations in return.

Effectuated by its own sense of grandeur, the Atrium strived to uphold the structural and social integrity, or conformity, on which it had long ago been fashioned. And uphold it, it did. Day in and day out, the walkers revered their host, complying with, relegating to, and lusting for its stern dictate. By all measures, it was a metro-human cultural symbiosis.

How ever dismal the walkers abetted the Atrium to be during the business day, it was a far more desolate place at night—so desolate, in fact, that no one ventured there at night, or, plausibly, so desolate, in fact, *because* no one ventured there at night. Arguably, the Atrium made no sound whatsoever at night, as it yielded to the metaphysical precept that there can be no sound without one present to hear it.

If one were present in the Atrium at night, which is naught in point, he would hear mostly the sound of his own breath over the faint hum of the frosted glass street lanterns strewn regularly along the protracted distances of the Atrium's imprisoning lanes. He might hear the wind blow, perhaps fancying that it chanted his name or whispered some delicate secret. Each and every of his footsteps would ring out like hard beats on a drum. His own voice would sound foreign to him, maybe like the voice of God, surrounding him and reducing him to but one seam in a never-ending column of grey space.

He would see little more than what he could hear. Those buzzing, dim lights would haze the Atrium's length and breadth out of both his central and peripheral views. Yet, he would irrefutably feel the Atrium's reign. He'd sense its empty sprawl around him in a brief flash before the tall buildings, above and beside him, closed down on him like a predator's bite upon its prey. He'd be trapped in the beast's otherwise empty belly, sloshed and churned with insipid chum.

Oh, he, the one who we can only imagine in the Atrium's nocturnal warren as none of sound mind would in fact be, he would be taunted by his presence there. What he could not hear, what he could not see, would blend with the perceptual fallacies he himself conjured with the Atrium's aid. This mix would toil at him in gushes, acid fluxing through pap. He'd feel ensnared in this wherever, whatever, to which he had fallen victim, yearning to escape.

Soon enough, he would be set free, puckered out through the series of smooth muscle contractions that concluded the beast's digestive process. When shat out in due course, he'd find himself a changed man, a mottled russet husk of all that he had once been—drained of whatever glimmer of vitality he formerly had, he would be reduced to noxious mush.

What an odd occurrence his nocturnal presence there would seem to be—for the very silence, the very hard-sketched disconnection and grey succor, he craved during the day would devour him at night.

That was one's juxtaposition in this town. He could not escape the inhered duality there—he was damned to con-sume that which, whether by day or by night, ultimately consumed him.

But damned he was through his own volition. To be sure,

his damnation was the eventual consequence of his daily routine: with each successful successive recession from human interaction and sensation, he inevitably quelled part before parcel of his own humanity.

These psychological constructs were as much a part of the town as its physical construction, the mental mortar to the town's buildings' bricks. The way that life played out was an outward manifestation, an imperfect reflection, of how the town had long ago been methodically laid out.

And what a layout it was! The Atrium itself housed only four buildings—the Bank, the Town Hall, the Sheriff's Station, and the Church—with one building seated in each corner of the Atrium's square lot. These four buildings sat close to each other and, by all literal means, were concretely connected to one another.

By the Atrium's construction, each building was visibly woven against the others by barbell patterns of brick inlay which bulged at each building's gut entrance and tapered off into two narrowly distinct sauntering paths, both of which equally but separately bled into the brick bulges encircling the adjacent and opposite buildings' doors. This set-up, call it one of ease and practicality or one of manipulative devise, quite tangibly indicated that there was no separation of church and state in this town.

The Church was on the Northeast corner. Although there were other churches in town, this was the only church at its center. It was a Presbyterian church, not nearly as ostentatious, inside or out, as its Catholic cousins found miles away.

Inside, the Church was mostly greyscale. Few things adorned the walls, only crosses and bland, linear religious art. Its exterior was the same stale concrete color as the Atrium's other buildings, and its shape was mostly the same as the other buildings.

Its shape departed from the Atrium's standard rectangular plan only by slight deviations found in the few mockingly out-of-place Baroque appendages and fixtures that punctuated the otherwise smooth grey space. First Presbyterian Church had few windows, proverbially permitting those whose religious fervor lived within to throw stones.

Still north, and west of the Church, the Town Hall ruled as the busiest building in the Atrium's quad. It contained all of the major bureaucratic town departments and judicial and legislative agencies and most of the white collar professional headquarters.

This one building employed more citizens than any other single building in the town could claim to employ. The typical employee seldom realized this since each room of the building was shut off from the others with locked doors tracts apart from each other. The honeycomb had been smashed, and the worker bees were trapped within.

South of this west, the red brick path led to the Sheriff's Station. The Station was the shortest and the least frequented of the four buildings. Only the sheriff and his deputies were regulars at this site. Most others avoided it whenever they could.

It was darker, warmer, and thicker than most other places. Even though it was above ground, it felt like a dank cellar at times. The lock-up cells were usually empty, except for the occasional drunk or prankster who'd caused a scene or for some unfortunate person with the wrong ideas who ended up in the wrong place at the wrong time.

The last building, the Bank, rested east of the Station and south of the Church. Though a typical bank, as per its bored tellers and ruthless loan officers and executives, the Bank was quite special merely for its decor.

It was fabulously decorated with tremendous, 5-foot-tall,

empty black lacquered vases, or urns, and dark green marble countertops accenting its warm pink walls and gold-trimmed beige sconces and table lamps. The tellers had lush leather chairs on which to plop their rotund behinds. The round, gold-plated door to the vault, which held colonies of safety deposit boxes protecting both citizens' valuables and a portion of the Bank's reserve, was always left open but fenced off by a wrought iron gate, some eight feet tall, behind which two security guards always stood at full attention.

Indeed, the Atrium was aptly named. These four buildings, on the four corners of this town's center, represented the four chambers of the town's communal heart. The lifeblood of this town was spawned by, and fed to, the blatant objectives of these four edifices—Money, Power, Control, and some form of God.

With only four buildings on the Atrium's plane, each pressed to one corner, the space between them seemed immense and tragically empty even when populated. At the axis of the Atrium's plot, at its geometric midpoint, a fountain had long ago run dry. Or, rather, its flow of water had long ago been cut off.

The fountain had a large concrete bowl base approximately twelve feet in diameter. At its middle, a 4-foot-tall concrete ball supported a plate half the size of the bowl beneath. Concrete curls tapered a yard up from one foot inward of the plate's circumference and narrowed to a peak on which another ball, likely 27 inches wide, crowned the large piece.

Other than rain, snow, or sleet, and occasionally, spit, vomit, or piss, no form of water had danced in this fountain for a few decades. Those who hadn't heard the lore of the fountain's glory past—visitors, young adult and child citizens, and new arrivals—or those who chose to forget were always perplexed by the large object at the Atrium's center.

Some considered it an intentional piece of art or historic preservation rounding out, in form and function, the Atrium's design. Others saw it as the bulleted handle of the town's roulette wheel.

From the Atrium, the town extended outward in six exponentially cascading tetragons precincted according to a home-is-where-the-heart-is ideal. The Atrium's four walls flushed to the four curbs of one street—Main Square. Although even the weakest eyes could easily discern from Main Square four separate streets pinched off by the Atrium's corners, it simply wasn't the case that these four streets were anything other than one. Main Square was one street—a street in a square course that enveloped the Atrium.

Main Square sat in front of two sets of four other streets. These back streets, however, were each given their own names. Eight streets named after eight former presidents, republicans for the most part. Each successive set of four streets comprised a box which was a little larger in area than the box before it.

Main Square and the presidential streets behind it were zoned only for commercial use. On these streets, one could find a myriad of places to eat, shop, and spend.

In each direction, a wide lane separated the last of the presidential streets from another awkwardly square street, First Square. First Square was purely residential, the only street in the entire town zoned solely for that purpose. And it was there that the most cherished citizens lived—those with the most money or the most prestige, those the town believed had the most reason to be there. A limited list of lawyers, doctors, bankers, clergy, and town officials—mainly, the upper echelon of the Atrium's institutions. There were only so many houses on First Square, all of them large and lovely and, therefore, so ridiculously priced that only those who actually lived there could ever afford to do so.

Behind First Square, there were four other sets of four streets which, like the presidential sets before them, each created a box a little larger in area than the box ahead. The four streets in these four sets had their own names, like Eureka, Baum, Temperance, Sharp, and so on.

Though predominantly residential, these streets were zoned for certain mixed uses. There were corner markets and diners here and there. A hospital. A K through 12 school. Two gas stations. St. Mark's Catholic Church.

But mostly houses. Nice houses, big houses. Pretty lawns. The people that resided in these houses were by and large professionals of some sort or another, maybe not the highest paid but still bringing home a fat slice of bacon, and occasionally well-paid paraprofessionals and aging trust fund babies.

Another square street—predictably tagged Second Square—tailed the other sides of the wide lanes in every direction at First Square's humblest four followers' hinds. Like First Square, Second Square had behind it four expanding sets of four streets, and each street in each set had its own lively name.

The remainder of the town's layout followed this scheme all the way out to Fifth Square, repeatedly carving out discrete cartons of neighborhood space that protracted with distance from the Atrium and broke into flights of contained occupancy by the succession of four-sided streets with numeric names.

On Second Square and the streets immediately behind it, mostly medium-sized houses and townhouses perched the land. Duplexes, condominiums, and two- or three- story apartment dwellings debuted on the streets behind Third Square and took center stage by Fourth Square. Past Fifth Square, there were very few houses, other than row houses, to be found. Back there, small apartments in large complexes were the norm.

From Second to Fifth Square, and beyond, the streets were pocked with enough businesses and facilities to keep one healthy, happy, and clean. The less favorable industries that every town needs in order to survive were located only beyond Fourth Square and mostly past Fifth. The psychiatric hospital, convalescent home, and dog pound, to name but a few necessary nuisances, were on streets cast between Fourth and Fifth Square.

Most folks 'round these parts would have claimed that the town ended somewhere past Fifth Square, that some of those single-line, unbending streets behind Fifth Square were on the outskirts of town. So it was okay for them folks to toss their trash that way. Out past Fifth Square—that's where the dump and the jail were. And too many people lived out there and had a real nice view of the trash—but most folks 'round these parts didn't too much think about them people.

Power and privilege were painstakingly choreographed along the town's geographic lines (or, rather, squares). In this town, you were where you lived and you lived what you were. Everyone was born into a certain position, geographically and socially.

The coloreds—the black people and the Hispanics who came from no one knows where—lived on Fifth Square and the streets behind. They never really lasted long inward past Third Square. An infant's handful of black families had made it to Second Square before—but only for a brief stint. Soon enough, somehow, someway, something happened to make the black family pack up and move even farther away from town than they had been before.

It wasn't all about race, though. It was also about class. Whites were separated from blacks and from other whites as well. First and Second Square were reserved for the white cream of the white crop. The lower class whites lived past

Third and Fourth Square. Some lived on Fifth Square and its ends—these were the backyard whites, likely there because they married outside of their race or one way or another ended up there by some act that was or wasn't anybody's fault but their own.

Nothing just happened out of the blue. The zoning plan and the real estate market, together, parented a town physically divided into distinct social cells through which very few ever diffused.

For the poor, there was little, if any, upward social mobility. All the accessible job markets were more or less capped and stalemated, whether because the human supply exceeded the labor demand or because dandy suits didn't want to dip into an oily pool of candidates of the wrong color or class.

For the rich, and for the not-so-poor, it was a different story. They had to watch everything they said and did—they had to protect themselves from what the respectable citizens thought—because, with one wrong move, they could lose everything they had. Once fallen, one could not, can not, climb back up.

Life in this town had been like this since anybody could remember. And it showed no signs of stopping. At the very least, the visual vestiges of the town's retained racism and classism would have been torn down decades ago in other towns. At the very most, other towns would have tapped into the town's groundwater to dam(n) the cyclic flow of these vulgar-isms. But not here—for this town was not like other towns. It was something altogether its own.

Most nobody here ever wondered whether the chicken or the egg came first. They thought the point was already moot. After all, they lived in a modern world where chickens abound and eggs are aplenty. There was no need to stress over which came first, because they both were here now. Each gave way to the other.

The chickens laid eggs that hatched into chickens, the eggs hatched into chickens that laid eggs, in this town. Sequence would become important only when the cycle was broken. And the cycle had not yet been broken here.

~ 2 ~

"Think about it for a little bit, Tad. You don't have to answer me right now. I know it's a lot to swallow… And, there's more I have to tell you. So just hear me out."

They had been sitting in a small diner this whole time. Larry's Last Stop. She was sipping a coffee, he an iced tea, throughout her oration.

Larry's, as most liked to call it, was a run-of-the-mill dive diner in this town. It sat proudly on Third Square, inviting patrons from all ends of the town's spectrum. It got equal shares of its business from dine-in and carry-out customers alike.

Normally, Larry's' commercial space was flooded with teenagers, young adults, and old folks. The teenagers and young adults swarmed there because it was a cool place to hang out. They could sit there for hours on end, just like she and Tad were doing tonight, without any strife for ordering nothing more than beverages with free refills.

The elderly liked Larry's for its quick service, affordable prices, and tasty food. Even though, as take-out customers, the grey-hairs would have had the same tasty food at the same affordable prices, there was something else that drew most of them there. In the main, the old folks who ate at Larry's were the widowed, the terminally single, and the terminally alone. Larry's was a place where they could eat a meal with other people even when they sat unaccompanied. They could be around the youth that had forsaken them.

When mourning met with old age in this town, something poignant usually happened. All those years that one had spent secluded from the others around him, those years he was paired only with a wife who died before him, with children who moved away or forgot him, or with a job from which he retired, gave him reason to regret. His hindsight was 20/20. He saw the errors of his ways, wishing he'd kept in touch with old friends or had meaningful discussions with coworkers.

He resented the fact that his usual company was a television whose technology perplexed him. On the remote control he struggled to understand, there was a "REWIND" button—how he sobbed when he discovered its true function.

Alone and alone, all he wanted was what he hadn't known before. The companionship of others, the sound of another voice or smell of another person outside of him and his immediate own, became his highest priority. Yet, set in his ways for far too long, he knew not how to directly achieve this. He was too familiar with dismissive salutations and turned glances to grab what he wanted.

Instead, he became a spectator on the outside of the interpersonal dealings he envied. He went to Larry's to watch what he could not have. Like the sympathy pains he felt when his wife was pregnant, he absorbed the feelings around him and tried to circumvent the realization that humanity, just like technology, may have progressed far beyond his comprehension.

Twenty or thirty years ago, he would have done as the majority of his junior mid-life reflections did now. The greater part of Larry's' take-out customers was comprised of persons falling somewhere between young adulthood and old age. They were the people who liked the tasty food at the affordable prices but disliked certain aspects of Larry's' operation.

Those from the better parts of town probably wanted to avoid the atmosphere and mix of people they considered below them. Those from the worse parts of town probably wanted a supper where they didn't have to leave a gratuity. All probably wanted to avoid the generations which sandwiched them, to evade the emblems of both the youth that'd abandoned them and the old age that chased them.

From time to time, despite Larry's' typical constituency, a few thirty- or forty- somethings, usually male, haphazardly happened in for more than take-out business. Each man came in alone, and sat alone, for a quick and quiet nip or nibble. Staring straight forward with a vacant look in his eyes, he sat oblivious to his surroundings like a mouth-breathing zombie dead to the living world.

He, like his middle-aged take-out counterparts, seemed motivated to sidestep contact with, or acknowledgement of, the symbols of his forgotten past and inevitable future. But, unlike his buy-and-fly peers, he was motivated by something else as well.

Eight hours a day, five days a week, he saw the same people and worked on the same projects at his place of employment. Six nights a week, he went to sleep in the same bed at the same hour and slept the same sleep. Twice, if he was lucky maybe three times, a week, he coupled with the same woman in the same sexual positions and same mechanical way. Same house. Same car. Same receding hairline. Life was boring. Day in and day out, nothing changed. And, he realized, it probably never would.

Maybe he sat in Larry's to sulk over how mundane his life truly was or to experience something different in a world where everything was the same. Or maybe he sat here because he'd forgotten to phone in his take-out order or was just passing by and had some free time to kill. Whatever the case, the occasional hour or two at Larry's was an intermission between the predictable parts of his daily life. Why he spent that break blank, wooly, and numb none could know for sure, not even he.

Thus those that lived life, coveted life, and paused life jumbled unblended in Larry's Last Stop, spread out over a seating area that was much longer than wide. Past the entrance, a file of twelve big booths flanked the right wall. Across from the booths, a school of stools lined the long counter in front of the bar and the kitchen doors. The older folks, and the glazed-over mid-lifers, usually sat at the counter to eat their lonely meals while the youths filled the booths with couples or small packs.

No matter where they stood, sat, or walked, Larry's' patrons were always cast in a dim yellow light that drew out all of the shadows, lines, and flaws on their physical entireties. The action in Larry's played out like the screening of an old 8mm film with too much contrast and sharpness and a saturated gloomy piss-colored tint.

In other words, the lighting in Larry's was bad. Each bulb had the same low wattage and teemed the same muted beam. The surprisingly thin plastic shades encircling each bulb were a pale mustard color darkened by decades of cigarette, cigar, and pipe smoke.

The bulbs and shades were set in light fixtures that dangled down from the ceiling over every other table and regularly over the counter such that six pairs of hanging lamps stretched from one end of the diner to the other. The hanging lights shone the heaviest and the hottest on those seated below them and radiated dim spheres that encroached slightly on the ends of the otherwise unlit neighboring booths or seats. The circles of light emanating from each dangling lantern, rather than colliding with or intersecting each other, polka dotted Larry's' landscape.

Underneath the things and people beneath the lights, Larry's' floor was checkered with large linoleum tiles from end to end. The tiles were black and white, but for one tile.

One tile was light blue.

A couple of years ago, Larry, the son of the original Larry's son Larry's son Larry, was replacing a caved-in booth seat when, much to his chagrin, he tore a large slash into one black square while moving the busted seat. Pam, the cliché head waitress, was quick to remedy the situation.

She and Carl, her in-house ex-husband, had recently re-floored the bathroom in their plebian-plush pad (the lower left half of an evolving triplex, which was far lower than left), and they had some extra linoleum left over—a slab of light blue linoleum that they'd been using as a placemat for their dog LumLum's food and water bowls.

Larry was a sensible man and could not turn down a quick and free solution, so he willingly accepted Pam's donation even though its color departed from his floor's theme. As for Pam, had she been a bit cleverer, she could have tried to declare the contribution as a deduction on her taxes.

Larry made no attempt to alter or hide the blue linoleum square. Rather, he just slapped it down on the floor and let its color wade the black and white around it. The blue square was not under any table or seat. It stood out, and hollered, in the open aisle between the booths and counter, lined up to the center of a booth's table two booths from the last. It was at this table that she insisted always to sit.

And it was at this table that she and Tad sat tonight.

"I know what I have to do, and I know when I'm going to do it. But, I'm not exactly sure how I want to do it yet, Tad. I've been thinking about it for a while. Considering all the options, I guess. There're plenty of them. I just need to find the one that works best for me."

Works best? I know what would work best—the one option she hasn't considered. Life. Living. She hasn't considered living. She's considered every option except the best one.

"The way I see it, it all boils down to one thing—the difference between escape and release… To escape is to leave a place of your own will, to break free from restraint. It's a selfish act. And, I don't mean selfish as in greedy or anything. I mean selfish like the person who escapes, and that person alone, is doing something for himself. He's doing it for his own self's preservation or protection, not for anybody else's. It's one self that acts for its self—one person is both the actor and the object of his actions.

"Release is a different thing though. When there's a release, it's one person letting another person free. The actor and the object of his actions are not the same—they're two different people. I guess you could say the actor is selfless, altruistic maybe, because he's doing something for the sake of another.

"Like, think of prison. When a prisoner escapes, he disobeys the system and acts on his own will because he wants to be free. But, when a prisoner's released, the system lets him go because he's served his time and deserves to be free. Now, I know that what a person wants and what a person deserves are two entirely different things sometimes, but I'm just using prison as an example… I'm sure you get the point."

Over two hours had passed since they first arrived at Larry's tonight. For that pair-plus of hours, they'd been parked beneath a thick circle of light, dog-eared by the blue linoleum square beside only them, and had ordered nothing but the beverages that sat before them.

Tad's iced tea and her coffee had seen numerous refill reincarnations of a glass and a cup that were never half empty and never half full. Pam saw to that—at regular intervals, she walked past their table and replenished their supplies of caffeinated, browned water.

With continuous frequent refills to a glass and a cup that were not ever emptied, neither she nor Tad could be certain how much of what they drank was fresh and how much had been there since their night's beginning.

Pam was able to be so attentive because Larry's wasn't too crowded right now. They'd arrived around 7:30 p.m., right after the dinner specials ended but before the late night crowd hit the scene. When they first got here, only three other booths were occupied and four lonesome men sat at the counter. In what seemed like no time, the three occupied booths were vacated as others were filled, balancing the loss of one patron with the gain of another, and the four lonesome men left the counter to go home to their lonesome wives and lonesome obligations.

Around 8:30, two young men stumbled in. They were familiar faces around her age, both novice loan officers at the Bank. One of the fellows dropped out of law school to pursue what he deemed a faster track to success. The other'd done little with his young life but was fortunate enough to be from one of the town's only Jewish families—and, since Jews are good with numbers and money, or so they in this town assumed, the Bank hired him although he had little education and no experience.

Both young men were wearing similar dark suits with loosened pastel ties and both were rather drunk. They'd gone out for drinks after work, no doubt, and obviously drank at least one too many by now. They sat side-by-side at the counter and swilled beer after beer as they patted each other on the back.

Pam looked the other way when these two chaps carried shots of whiskey to the three teenaged girls who'd caught their eyes from a booth across the way. A little bit later, Pam shook her head in defeat when the girls slipped on their high school cheerleading jackets, in which they'd earlier perspired after cheerleading practice this evening, and walked out encircled by the spaghetti arms of these blokes.

Their brief drunken presence in Larry's made it seem like a bar for a bit. And the two letters on the girls' jackets—the large capital "J" and the large capital "V" on each—evinced a delirious routine too many too often were too anxious to follow or too eager to lead.

It was after 10:00 now. Though Larry's wasn't as congested as it would be in another hour or so, business was starting to pick up. It'd been a while since Tad last sipped his iced tea. Nonetheless, his right hand was wrapped tightly around the glass and his thumb consistently caressed the cold film of water that had accumulated on the outside of the glass. He pressed his lips to the straw, drew in a mouthful of the cool tea, swallowed, and then bit his tongue as she continued her address.

~ 3 ~

"In a lot of ways—in almost every way that matters—human mortality is the ultimate exercise of these principles… Every person's death is either an escape or a release."

She's prefaced her thoughts about life and death on something best exemplified by prison. Is that what life is to her? Is this world, her life, nothing but a prison?

I wonder how she got here then. What her crime had been. Who'd pointed his finger at her. Who'd sentenced her to this penal complex. Whether she'd been unjustly condemned.

Tad's mouth was still fixed to the straw, and he swallowed several large gulps of iced tea as his mind wandered. All the same, his mouth was very dry. He pressed his tongue to the roof of his mouth. It felt like every drop of fresh lemon juice he'd squeezed into his glass gathered there, "Every death is either an escape or a release?"

"Right… See, most people believe that man has both a body and a soul and that the body can only live for so long but that the soul can live forever. So, if humans are truly integrated beings, this means that each individual human life actually represents two lives playing out together—the life of the body and the life of the soul. The body and the soul simultaneously live their lives as one gestalt unit until the body dies.

"It's like that phrase 'two sides of the same coin.' Man is a coin, Tad. His body is one side of the coin and his soul is the other… But, coins are three dimensional—there's something between a coin's two sides. There's a middle that holds them together and makes the coin larger than the sum of its two sides. That's why man's corporeal existence, like a coin, is a gestalt unit… So, it kind of makes you wonder—when the body dies, when one side of the coin is chopped off or peeled away, what happens to all that stuff in the middle?"

Her hair flooded down over her shoulders and covered most of her back. The long brown waves seemed motionless as she spoke.

Tonight, she wore her hair in one of the only two hairstyles she'd ever known. Tonight, her untamed mane was tucked behind her ears and pushed to the back. On a different night, it might be ironed out and pulled to a taut ponytail at the bottom of her crown. But that would be a different night.

Between these two hairstyles she would shift, choosing one or the other based on the nature of where she was going, who she was going with, or what she was trying to accomplish for herself. Wild hair tucked behind her ears was her "casual" style—the way she wore it when she did the ordinary and usual things in life.

Wild hair tucked behind her ears when she went to the grocery store. Wild hair tucked behind her ears for a casual night with friends. Wild hair tucked behind her ears to go for a walk. Wild hair tucked behind her ears tonight, though tonight was no ordinary and usual night.

Her other style, she reserved for "special occasions." Parties, holidays, town events—whenever she wanted or needed to feel pretty.

There was an obvious difference between her two hairstyles. Wild and tucked, her hair drew attention away from her face while the tight tamed ponytail seemed to draw out all of her fine features. But the difference was in something more than just her appearance. It was an overall difference in her attitude. The latter gave her confidence. The former gave her comfort. It was a great shame that neither could give her both.

She had a long face—a narrow oval, as far as faces go.

Her nose was small and delicate. It had on it only one small bump, from where it had been broken during high school softball practice about a decade ago.

How she hated that little bump on her nose. Although no one else ever noticed it, she knew it was there. She didn't mind having an imperfection. In fact, she had more than a few of them. What bothered her about the bump on her nose was not the fact that it was there but how it got there.

Ten years ago, she decided to join the high school softball team even though she had never played softball before. Margo didn't like the idea of her playing softball. Margo told her not to join the team. Margo warned her, in precise terms, "Don't join the softball team! You don't know how to play! You could get hurt—you could break your nose!"

Scene: second softball practice of the season; she steps up to the plate; the ball is thrown; she misses; her unlikely ally, the catcher behind, a girl named Tracy Lynn, offers a suggestion, "Wait three seconds longer, then swing;" the ball is out there; one; two; three; fade to black. End scene.

One, two, three, the softball struck her in the face. One, two, three, what had Margo said? "You could get hurt—you could break your nose!"

"You could get hurt—you could break your nose!"

One, two, three. She went to the hospital. Her nose was broken.

After this happened, she took on a strange practice. Every time Margo would say something off-kilter—every time Margo would suggest that some action might have some undesirable or drastic outcome—she would tell Margo to "Take it back!" She'd bark her demand over and over again until Margo said four simple words: "I take it back."

If Margo said any more, or any less, than these four words, or if she said any derivation of these words or spoke in lulled, inaudible, or, even, sarcastic terms, she'd go into a fit until Margo said it right or said it again, "I take it back."

This was a necessary practice for her. When Margo told her not to play softball because she might break her nose, she never told her to take it back. And that, that, of course, is why she broke her nose.

In no way did she believe that Margo had any type of psychic or paranormal power. She knew Margo wasn't predicting the future or setting a curse. But Margo was putting words and ideas out there. And those words and ideas, once out there, might end up spilling the water that would cause that inevitable physical Freudian slip. Margo's warnings would dominate her thoughts, those at the forefront and those dormant alike, indirectly leading her to whatever downfall Margo mentioned.

Margo's words and ideas would latch on to her like an obnoxious tail and follow her wherever she went. In telling Margo to "Take it back," she was telling Margo to yank her tail off so that the words and ideas wouldn't follow her around all day. She was telling Margo to take back the words and ideas she'd put in the world—to remove them from thought

One, two, three. It was amazing that she believed this was somehow possible.

"You could get hurt—you could break your nose." That damn bump!

It came to symbolize so many things in her life.

One: Margo never anticipated anything good or great for her. All Margo saw for her was an ill fate—destruction and pain, terrible outcomes to even the most benign acts.

Two: She herself came to fear everything she did. She came to contemplate those dreadful outcomes even before Margo spoke of them. Her own fear inhibited a lot of her tendencies. She'd become afraid of life and living.

Three: When some of those outcomes about which Margo warned, and she herself feared, came to fruition, she saw that there were some things that would occur despite her efforts at prevention. She realized that she was the only thing she could control in this world, not other things or other people.

One, two, three. That bump reminded her that Margo, her fear, and chance were all working against her efforts at a happy life. That damn bump damned her.

On either side of her bumped nose was a pale blue eye, usually accented with the most precise and perfect of eye makeup. Always black eyeliner and always black mascara. For her lips, she regularly preferred a burgundy lipstick carefully smoothed on.

Her long neck stemmed her long, oval face and tapered down to her round shoulders. Her body was full and plump. She was a curvy girl with some extra baggage to spare. She usually wore clothes that accentuated her womanly wares but hid most everything else. Tops that were tight around her breasts but flowing over her belly. Pants that were firm at the rear but wide at the legs. All attire always some shade of black, brown, or dark blue.

Tonight was no different. She wore a worn-in black V-neck shirt that hugged her chest and draped down over the rest of her torso. Wide-leg brown pants that tied in the front. And black suede sandals. She always wore black suede sandals—year-round, with or without socks depending on the season.

She had a white gold watch on her left wrist, as usual. To her, this watch had no significance or meaning other than Time. The only other piece of jewelry she wore was a yellow gold chain with a flat, round charm dangling at its end.

She wore this necklace every day. She'd worn it every day of her life since the day of her sister's burial, when the funeral home director handed it to her among her sister's other final personal effects. When he gave it to her, it was zipped up in a little green pouch bearing the name and contact information of the funeral home. She unzipped the pouch, pulled out the necklace, and slipped it over her head.

Since then, it was a fixture on her neck. There were times when she took it off. But she never kept it off. She'd change it out for a set of pearls for a formal affair—but as soon as she got home from the affair, it was straight back to her necklace. In all those years since her sister's death, the necklace was never off of her neck for more than several hours at a time.

"I know I'm getting a little off track, but bear with me… For man, maybe the middle is a mess of everything he was, is, and could be—a collective memory of all his earthly experiences and emotions, a collective drive of all his ethereal dreams and desires. While the body and soul live together, that middle's something denser, more tightly packed, than either side alone. It's something his body and soul share… But, it's all mixed together. It can't be easily divided down the center because what one side contributes to the mix the other side uses. What the soul wants can influence how the body acts. What the body experiences can influence what the soul needs.

"Now, I'm sure you noticed that what I just said about the middle of man's coin is a little circular. And, I suppose it should be. After all, Tad—coins are round… But, my point is that I think the middle attaches to the soul. Like petals to a flower's center—pinched oblong reactions that grow out from one point and each end where they all started.

"I guess you could say that man's middle is his mind… So, it's the mind that attaches to the soul. But, even though the mind attaches to the soul, while the body's alive, the soul can't claim the mind as its own because it needs the body's contributions to shape the mind. Like, the mind uses the body's actions and thoughts to complete the soul's functions—the body provides the semi-circles of the soul's reactions, the arcs from which the mind carries feedback to the soul.

"At the moment the body dies, the mind rounds out a final reaction—and, since the soul no longer needs the body's input for definition and the body no longer needs the mind, the soul can finally take complete possession of the mind. Two lives of body and soul are reduced to one that was fattened by the other.

"After death, the soul carries the mind with it wherever it goes… And, that's how we can still be ourselves when we go to heaven or hell. That's how our families and friends recognize us when we die and meet them again; that's how God knows who we are—it's not by the faces and bodies that can't exist in heaven. It's by our minds, the energy of our middles, the earthly memories our souls take with them."

Tad was a good-looking young man. He had a well-defined face, with deep-set hazel eyes and a severe nose cast between. His lips were full and smooth. Not quite pink, but not quite red. Plump. He had the kind of lips that some girls long to bite. But not her. She never longed to bite his lips. *She never tried to take my lower lip into her mouth, bite hard, and pull away. Never tried to rip my flesh like some estranged canine might. Never.*

On an off day, there might be a shadow of hair dancing above his top lip—maybe some spot he'd missed when shaving that day, or maybe some spot from where hair just happened to frequently sprout.

His hair was dark brown. It bordered on black. It was mostly short, but longer on the top. Not long like a girl's hair, of course. Just as long as his fingers, that's all. He had a 2-inch-long horizontal scar on the back of his neck. He had fallen off of a swing many, many years ago and cut his neck pretty badly on the tossed-aside plastic lunchbox which landed his fall.

On this night, he was dressed the same as every other night. A tee shirt and jeans, both too big for him. At 6'1", he was quite lean weighing in at only 157 pounds. He liked his clothes to hang off of him a bit, to give a little yield.

Tonight, the tee shirt was blue and the jeans were only slightly frayed at the cuffs. There was a hole in his back right pocket. A tiny one—not so bad that things would fall out but big enough to catch notice. His white low-top sneakers were rather scuffed.

He owned neither a watch nor a wallet. Money was always held loosely in his front pockets—and, yes, those front pockets sometimes had holes that, unlike the one on the back of his pants tonight, allowed piece by piece of money, and the occasional photo ID, to slither down his thigh, over his calf, down the laces of his shoes, and onto the ground, where some other person, some stranger or some acquaintance, would later take adverse possession without the slightest tinge of moral consequence.

Tad's refusal to wear a watch was founded on one simple ground. He didn't like the way it felt on his wrist. Leather would cause his skin to sweat or to chafe. And metal always felt too cold, or too hot, in any given weather.

No, Tad did not seek to abandon Time. He did not seek to follow natural rules rather than prescription. He merely didn't like the way watches felt on his skin. So he never wore one. *Plus, there's a clock most everywhere you go nowadays.*

"When the soul claims the mind and leaves the body, it usually does so by one of two means—escape or release. The body, or God, either lets the soul go or the soul leaves on its own.

"I guess when a person dies a natural death or what-ever—whenever he dies by an accident or by the force of nature—it's a release. It's like God looks at the living person as a unit and sees a body that's old and decrepit, ridden with some disease or disorder, or mauled and wounded by some outside event. But, he sees this living soul still fused to the dying body. So, he intervenes—he speaks to the gestalt unit. By telling the entire unit that its body's done with its time on earth and its soul is free to move on, God releases the soul from its connections to the body. The soul is set free. And, the body dies.

"But, there are so many people in this world, and God's a busy man. He doesn't have the time to make sure that every release happens when it should. He can't tend to every dying body at one time, so he frequently schedules appointments… You know, like people who have terminal illnesses or some other condition where their bodies are decaying more and more each day—like when a doctor tells a man he has only a few months or weeks to live, for whatever reason.

"Sometimes, when a person hears this kind of news, he doesn't want to wait for his appointment with God… Some-times, he'll take matters into his own hands… His mind is full of reactions that tell him his body's dying and his soul has somewhere else to go—eventually. He realizes this, and it's like his body starts to feel bad for his soul. His body knows that its time is coming and that his soul is more or less trapped until that time. So, his body kills itself to let his soul find heaven a little earlier than God had planned… His body gives up its life for the sake of his soul. His soul is set free. And, his body finishes dying… This too is a release, Tad.

"Now, there are some people who want their bodies to die even though they aren't dying. And, for these people, death is something else… For these people, the death of their bodies equates the escape of their souls.

"In this kind of situation, the man's soul is ready to live its own independent life in heaven even though his body isn't ready to quit living on earth. So, in order to be free, his soul must escape from the gestalt unit—and, to do so, his soul must kill his body… His soul starts by taking control of his mind, sending very specific messages through his middle. At some point, it's like his soul and his mind become one weapon that can overpower his body—together, they can act against his body and use his limbs to carry out their goal, to kill his body and escape together as one."

Tad sat leaning back against the booth so that his shoulders touched the top of the seat, his flat glut a few inches away from the seat's back. His right foot rested atop his left knee. His left hand on his lap, his right arm stretched out and bent across the top of the booth.

They seemed to be sitting in parallel lines. Her trunk's angle of recline was similar to his, plotted a few positive integrals away in a tertiary dimension. *As if mirrored.* As he was reclined back against the seat, she was leant forward over the table. Her hands were clasped somewhere near the center of the table, and her ample chest rested in the nest created by her arms.

"I think that's what's happening to me… It feels like my soul and my mind have become one. My mind's an ingrown hair on my soul, Tad… My soul's taken control and wants me to kill my body so it can move on… I'm not my body any more, Tad. I'm my soul. Can you see it? Can you see that I've become my soul? I have.

"Really, I have… And, I need to escape from my body… That's what I've been trying to figure out—the best way to escape. There're lots of ways to kill your body. I want to do it the right way."

Right way? There is no right way. If I slap her, will she

come out of this daze? If I scream at the top of my lungs, will she wake up?

She leaned back and brought her left hand to her mouth to chew on the tip of her middle finger, "It's going to be great, Tad. Believe me."

Just then, Larry's' door flung open and in walked an older lady dressed in shabby clothes and carrying two canes, one in each hand.

"Oh, Tad… Look. It's Alice. I'd hate to end up like that."

~ 4 ~

Alice. Alice Worth. Alice Worth was 60 years old. Among her many present and past titles were town cripple, town loon, occasional town drunk, and former town whore. But forty years ago she was just Alice. Alice, daughter, only child, of Dr. and Mrs. Samuel Worth of the First Square Worths.

Alice spent the opening twenty years of her life on First Square and enjoyed all of the privileges that ensued from her family's status and situs. But soon, things started to change in Alice's life. She stopped feeling normal, and strange things were happening to and around her.

Voices warned her to keep watch, for she was being hunted. Everyone, including her parents, was studying her and plotting behind her back. Her skin would turn purple, the voices said, whenever she neared a trap that her hunters had set.

Televisions and radios were monitoring her behavior as well. There was only one way to avoid being recorded: she had to place tiny balls of aluminum foil between the tops of her ears and skull and wrap bands of folded aluminum foil around both of her wrists and around her right thumb. The foil, they said, would also protect her from the radioactive waves that government officials emit when addressing the public and would allow her to travel to any place or any time in her mind.

For a while, Alice was able to keep her practices and concerns hidden from her family and the public—after all, it was they who hunted her, and she did not want them to know that she knew. But, in time, people started asking about the aluminum foil and wondering how Alice could claim to've been to Egypt, Switzerland, and Spain without having ever actually left town.

Her parents took her to the hospital, where, for two days, she underwent numerous physical and psychological tests. The diagnosis was schizophrenia. The suggested treatment was institutionalization for an indeterminate amount of time and 25 to 30 sessions of electroshock therapy.

The hospital staff released Alice into her parents' care, recommending that they take her home, keep her under constant supervision, spend some time with her, and then commit her to the psychiatric hospital. Alice did not want to be institutionalized. She did not want to receive electroshock therapy. She did not like her parents watching her.

She looked at her skin, and it was purple. Indeed, these were the traps they'd set for her. They'd had this in mind all along. She realized she'd been caught. But she wasn't going to surrender without a fight.

Late that night, while her mother slept soundly in bed and after her father dozed off in the chair outside of her door, Alice ran away. She didn't take many things with her, since she believed her parents probably installed tracking devices in her belongings. All she took with her was one change of clothes and $300 in cash.

When Alice's parents discovered she'd run away, there was little they could do about it. Alice was an adult—free to make her own decisions—and she ran away before she'd been committed or ordered to serve time in the loony bin.

For the first two or three months, the Worths would drive around town searching for Alice and, when they'd spot her, drive around following her for hours upon hours each day. Some of their close friends would follow Alice on foot some-times, to see where she was going or what she was doing, and report back to the Worths.

Following someone who felt hunted, studied, and plotted against probably wasn't the best idea. Alice saw the cars and pedestrians following her—her suspicions were yet again confirmed. She'd expended the first couple months of her getaway wandering around the town's proper streets, sleeping in alleys or entranceways, and spending what little money she had only on cigarettes and food. Since she was being hunted again, she decided to run further back to the town's farthest reaches.

She ended up out past Fifth Square. Her parents didn't know anyone that lived or worked out there, so there'd be none to follow her. And her parents probably wouldn't think to drive out this far to look for her—even if they did, this poor area was rich with alcoves and tight passageways between buildings, and a maze of rubbish mounds, in which she could hide.

Alice's money was gone in no time. She wasn't able to buy cigarettes or food anymore. The restaurants and gas stations whose bathrooms she used as toilets and makeshift baths refused her needs since she was no longer a paying customer. She was hungry, dirty, fixing for nicotine, and without money.

Alice turned her life to the dump. She explored it regularly to find her life's necessities. She unburied discarded clothing and shoes. She found cigarette butts and old magazines. Daily, she searched for rotten, stale, or moldy food that was pliable and viable enough for her to eat. When her discoveries were covered with maggots or bugs, she took it as a good thing—she'd smash the bugs between her fingers and eat them. Smashed, both so that she didn't have to chew them and so that they wouldn't be living inside her.

Alice also started sleeping in the dump. Usually, she'd sleep in one of the old cars that had been abandoned there—but sometimes, since she didn't want to remain in any one place for too long lest someone discover her, she'd find an old mattress or chair on which she'd cover herself with refuse and rest. It was in the dump that Alice found her professional calling.

When one of the refuse workers discovered her sleeping in her favorite old car, he threatened to call the police. Alice begged him not to call the cops and told him that she'd been hiding there because her parents and everyone else had been scheming to torture and kill her. The worker felt bad for her and agreed not to call the police. Alice asked him if the dump needed any more workers, if he could help her get a job. He was willing to help. He had a job in mind—not one he could get her, but one she could give him.

Thus Alice began her career as a whore. She performed various sexual acts with interested refuse workers, and whatever clientele they brought to the site, in exchange for money, cigarettes, or food.

Alice didn't make a grand living by any means. For each act she performed, she got a measly payout—if she was lucky, her customer would give her his brown bag lunch or an entire pack of cigarettes. She wasn't usually lucky though. On average, she only got a sandwich, maybe a cupcake, or three or four cigarettes. When she got cash, it was typically $5 or less. But Alice would take whatever she could get.

She soon decided to expand her operations. The jail was nearby—it had a large outside area at its back that was completely fenced in by latticed chain-link fencing from the ground to the roof. Every afternoon following lunch, the prisoners were given an hour of time outdoors. Alice went to the prison one day to sell her services.

Standing on one side of the fence, she called an inmate over to the other and offered him whatever sexual favor he wanted in exchange for a few cigarettes. He shoved every inch of himself that he could through one of the lattice holes in the fence. She dropped to her knees to earn her fee.

A guard saw what was happening and interrupted Alice's work. But the guard was a crooked man, in more than one way, and worked out a deal with her: she could come to the fence any time she wanted and service the inmates for compensation if she'd also service him, or any other guard, for free. Well, it wasn't for free per se—it was in exchange for the guards' allowing her to do this.

From that day on, Alice went to the fence to perform for cigarettes or whatever food items the prisoners could pocket from their recent lunches. There was usually a line of men standing at the fence, facing outward, waiting for her—sometimes maybe twenty men stood there, sometimes maybe five. The guard was always first in line. Down the line, she'd work, straining whichever part of her body her client requested against the lattice holes of the fence. She worked as much of the daily outdoors hour as she could, taking on as many consumers as time would allow.

She never walked the streets to sell her wares. But if someone walking or driving the road offered, she'd usually oblige. These were frequently cash transactions, more often than not a mere pittance. She'd also met some men that lived in the apartment buildings close by—she coupled with them in exchange for access to their apartments. Maybe they'd let her sleep on the floor one night, grant her access to the shower, or let her watch television for a couple hours.

For twelve years, Alice lived this way. Earning just enough cigarettes, food, money, and brief household experiences from the dump, the jail, and the streets, Alice was comfortable even though she was worse off than she'd ever been. She no longer felt hunted. Instead, she felt wanted, and proud that she could support herself in a world she thought would not support her.

But after twelve years, Alice's career abruptly ended.

She was in the dump late one night, acting on the friend of a friend of a friend of one of the legitimate dump employees, when things took an awful turn.

This man had pulled his truck up into the dump and parked behind a mound of trash. He was told Alice would be there, but he didn't know if he'd pulled up behind the correct heap. So he searched for Alice for nearly twenty minutes before he found her and brought her back to his truck to commission her work.

After his needs had been satisfied and he pulled up his pants, he reached over to his glove compartment to get his wallet and pay Alice. When he opened the glove compartment, however, his wallet was not there. He checked the back pocket of his recently removed and redressed pants. It was not there.

He shouted at Alice. He demanded that she tell him where his wallet was. She was confused and scared. She claimed she hadn't seen his wallet and didn't know what he was talking about.

He accused her of stealing his wallet. He insisted that she had set him up, that she must have been hiding near or in the trash when he'd pulled up and waited for him to go looking for her so that she could rob his truck. Alice denied this. But he did not believe her. He knew, he downright knew, she had stolen his wallet, and he wanted it back. The more she denied it, the more infuriated he became.

When she wouldn't fess up and tell him where his wallet was, he punched her in the face. Repeatedly, he punched her in the face, screaming and demanding his wallet. He punched over and over again.

Hard and fast, his balled right fist, with his thumb poking out between his four other fingers, slammed against her nose, eyes, and jaw. Blood was squirting out of the holes in her face, the ones that had already been there and the ones his thumbnail was now creating.

Bones, teeth—cracking. Alice cried at the top of her lungs. She begged for mercy until she couldn't cry any more. Even after her pleas and whimpers stopped, even after she was, apparently, unconscious, he continued to beat her. He relentlessly struck her face until his frustrations were gone.

When she had been conscious, she'd tried to fight him off—to no avail, she was a moving target. But now, limped and cataleptic, she was a bull's-eye for his aggression. As he cuffed her face over and over again, it had to've felt like hammering knotted clay; something so dense but so malleable giving way and caving to his tremendous force, not breaking with his blows but receiving and engulfing them.

He and his truck's interior were covered in blood by the time he finished with Alice. He knew she was still alive but thought her death was certain. He tore off her shirt to wipe his hands and arms clean and to sop up some of the blood that had pooled in the truck's cabin. Once clean, he got out of the truck, went to the other side, and ladled up her body and chucked her and her bloodied shirt atop a molehill of garbage.

When he got back into the driver's seat of his truck, he stepped on something hard. His wallet. Apparently, it'd fallen out of his pants' pocket, likely when his pants were down around his ankles as Alice pleasured him. He drove off and left her there to die.

She didn't die though.

Early the next morning, a refuse worker, one of her regular clients, found her and called the paramedics—though, he probably did not actually know that the victim he'd found was Alice. Her face was so bruised and broken that it had swollen to nearly double its size. Her eyelids were so enflamed that the crusted slits her eyeholes had become were barely visible. The butt of her nose was sideways against her right cheek and her lips bulged turgid over most of her lower face. Her four front teeth, and her upper left eye tooth, had been cleanly knocked out of her mouth. Her skin had turned purple.

She was rushed off to the hospital where, serendipitously, her father was the attending physician. She was a comatose Jane Doe for a few weeks before her father recognized some of her dislodged features.

Her attacker, her client, had beaten her so brutally that her left eye exploded in its socket and was nearly crushed to pulp. This eye was dead long before the paramedics ever recovered her. His roughness had partially detached the retina from her other eye and, as her eyes were inaccessible, due to severe swelling, at the most vital stages of her hospital stint, her retinal vascular bed ridged as blood vessels grew on her retina. The doctors could not intervene in time to stop the extraretinal neovascularization that completely detached her retina. By the time they accessed her broken right eye, the detached retina had adhered to the back of her lens, making her lens appear white and paling her already pale eye. Alice ended up being blind in both eyes—one dead, one living in compromised condition, neither would ever see again.

She was still in a coma when her father realized his patient was his daughter. Daily, he checked in on her as a doctor and as a father. Her mother sat at her side throughout the ordeal. When she awoke from her slumber, her parents tried to reason with her. They talked her into plastic surgery to fix most of her face and into receiving medicine, Haldol, for her psychological condition.

Although Alice had corrective surgeries to reset her nose and refurbish her shattered cheek- and face- bones, she refused any prostheses. She would not wear a partial dental plate to fill her gap of missing teeth. Instead, the gap remained unfilled in her mouth. She would not wear a glass eye in the empty socket on her left. Instead, she had her left eyelids sewn together, forever shut, and wore a patch over her lids' union.

Alice spent a long time in the hospital. When she fully recuperated and acclimated to her new psychiatric drug and treatment, she was released from the hospital and went home with her parents. She was in a helpless condition, blind and dependent on others with whom she hated to live.

Alice constantly beseeched her parents to let her leave their home but they would not allow it. She threatened that, if they didn't discharge her, she would either kill herself or run away again. If she did the latter, she assured them, she'd end up back on the streets and would probably die.

The Worths eventually acquiesced to her pleas and made arrangements for Alice to live in a first-floor apartment behind Third Square. They agreed to pay her monthly rent and employ an agent of the landlord to shop for Alice's groceries, pick up Alice's prescriptions, and intermittently tend to Alice's other household needs. They stipulated only that she continue to take her medication and visit a psychiatrist at least monthly.

Alice moved into that apartment and let that landlord's agent help her out. She kept taking her medication and seeing a psychiatrist regularly. Both blind and lucid for the first time in her life, Alice had a lot to get used to. She used a blind cane, in her right hand, when she walked—but still yet she often bumped into things or people and sporadically tripped or fell.

Sometimes, she crossed a street when she shouldn't have and nearly got hit by a car or a bike. She slept whenever she wanted and left her apartment whenever she desired, frequently sleeping through the day and spending nights awake and alone in her apartment or hiking on dark streets to restaurants or bars that had closed long before she even woke up. It was as if she'd lost the concept of time and was unwilling to find it again.

The crueler people in town had a field day with Alice's condition. Pranksters would move her blind cane away from where she'd placed it when she sat down on a bench. They'd steal food off of her plate just for fun's sake, not out of hunger, when she dined in public. So that she'd swat at the air around her or be startled, they'd lightly tap her on the shoulder without announcing or confirming their presence.

There were some who played even worse jokes on her. Like the cashiers or waitresses who short-changed her or fibbed about the denominations of money she handed them. Like the trio of boys who seduced her into a most disgraceful act of sodomy—one had preyed on her frailty and want of affection; he told her that he lusted after her and wanted to be with her. He took her back to his apartment, his two friends with him unbeknownst to her, and asked her for a blow job, "Don't use your hands, Alice. I'll put it in your mouth, don't worry. Just suck it." Alice never realized that he and one of his friends had hoisted his Great Dane to stand in an upright position where her partner was supposed to stand.

Too many people pulled the wool over Alice's blind eyes, and she was none the wiser. She simply never adapted to her impaired condition. Even after years of being blind, she still stumbled and confused hours. She was still the victim of malicious jokes.

She started drinking heavily, which only made everything worse. When she was about 45 years old, she fell down a flight of town steps—a flight she'd traversed many times, many times drunk, a flight of twenty steps. She broke her right hip. After some time in the hospital, she returned to her apartment. From then on, she walked with a limp.

By her 49th birthday, both of her parents had died—both of natural causes, old age, at different times but close enough to each other. They'd set up a solid trust fund for Alice's support. A bank official was to pay her rent each month, deliver to her account an allowance, and pay her landlord's agent a monthly stipend to both compensate the agent and finance Alice's groceries, medications, and necessities.

With Alice's parents out of the way, there was no one to whom the agent was accountable. The agent religiously abused the stipend, regularly providing Alice with inadequate amounts and types of food or toiletries. Alice was often hungry for days before the agent delivered more food. Her ass was often caked with feces because the agent hadn't purchased enough toilet paper and didn't spend a red cent on other paper products such as napkins, tissues, or paper towels.

She fell down too many times to count over the years. Each fall aggravated her broken hip until she needed a mobile cane to walk. That was how she ended up walking with two canes. She carried her mobile cane in her right hand, since that was the side on which her broken hip had been exasperated. In her left hand, she carried her blind cane. Sometimes, she got confused and waved her mobile cane around, since she'd used to carry the blind one in her right hand—those times she leaned down on her blind cane, she fell and usually broke the cane. She'd gone through too many blind canes that way.

To this day, Alice lived in this situation, still dumbfounded by her condition. Still drunk, hungry, or dirty from time to time. At 60 years old, her parents, whom she couldn't stand anyway, were long dead. She didn't have any friends. Most of the townspeople didn't talk to her anymore, unless she was on the paying end of a transaction. She was completely and utterly alone yet she woke up every day, got out of bed every day, and wandered through town every day. Every day.

Alice had a busted body—she couldn't see and couldn't

walk with ease. She had no one with whom to interact, no one with whom to enjoy life. Her world had to've been a thick, empty darkness. But, nonetheless, she navigated through it.

If Alice can, why can't she?

~ 5 ~

"I mean it, Tad. I'd hate to end up like Alice. That's got to be so horrible. There's so much to see in this world. But, Alice isn't able to see it."

And neither is she.

She turned her head and glanced over at Alice. Tad fixed his eyes on her to observe her as she observed. He wondered what it was about Alice's fate that she so feared. Was it just Alice's blindness? Alice's limited mobility or missing teeth? Or was it Alice's overall condition—the fact that Alice was alive and living?

Tad moved his stare to Alice. They both watched as Pam handed Alice a menu and walked away. Alice didn't flinch at Pam's cold shoulder; instead, she ran her hands over the menu repeatedly. But Alice was blind, and the menu wasn't in brail—so how was she to read it?

"I'm so afraid of ending up like her, so afraid of what the world might do to me in time. That's another good reason to leave, I guess."

No. It's a reason to live. Time could help her. Time could help her fix whatever it is she, not the world, has done to herself. She could use time to see more of this world, to stop being so scared.

Tad's stomach growled. At first, he fancied it growling at her—some primitive shout faintly flouting her flawed frontal brain flow. But no, it wasn't growling at her. It merely rumbled because it was not full. He hadn't eaten much today. A bowl of cereal when he woke up around noon. A small sack of potato chips he picked up at a local convenience store when he did his rounds about town in the late afternoon.

He had intended to order a sandwich, probably a grilled cheese, when he met up with her earlier this evening. But he never ordered it. He never had the chance. When they first arrived at Larry's, she said she wasn't hungry. Tad's set of manners, and awkward sense of self pride, prevented him from ordering food when his companion would not. Unlike a faction of Larry's' patrons, Tad refused to eat alone unless he was actually alone.

Plus, once their conversation, her oration, started, he completely lost his appetite. Yet, his stomach still turned over even though his mind overturned his hunger. His stomach growled once more. And, this time, she heard it.

She raised her right eyebrow, giggled, and then continued.

"I think about everything that can happen to a person— how we all get old and we all get sick. I don't want to end up like that. I don't want to wait for my liver to fail or my legs to go limp. I like things the way they are now. I want to be like this forever, and I will be. I'll be 26 years old forever, Tad. I'll be young and healthy. Not some widow or some cripple. I'll never need a dialysis machine or blood thinner. I'll never have to watch what I eat. I won't get sick and die like they did."

Tad knew what she was talking about. He knew about her past, about the lives and deaths of her parents and her sister. Though he'd never met them, he knew what happened to them—she'd told him all about it, just like she'd told him all about almost everything else in her life.

They'd spent many nights seated here, in this town, in this restaurant, in this booth, engulfed in whatever narrative she selected for a particular evening. He was an encyclopedia of her knowledge.

He knew. He knew about all the things that killed her family, what things her genes might carry, and he understood why those things might, and did, scare her. But he also knew that they hadn't killed her yet and that they might not ever.

Sure, if she lives, she might get sick like they did. She might die like they did. But she'll never know that if she stops living.

She's overlooked so much. The possibility that her genes are different. Medicine. Preventative care. Technological advances, medical breakthroughs. The prosthetics Alice refused!

Such focus on what life could take from her and not on what death would rob her of. She'd never eat again, never breath. She'd have no liver, no legs. No kidneys. No life. She'd be dead.

"That's the only thing we can be sure of, Tad—that we'll get old and sick and die. Like they say, from the moment you're born you start dying. It's torture, really. The worst kind there is. We're nothing more than time bombs, waiting to explode. Tic Toc. Tic Toc… We all know it's gonna happen. We just don't know when."

Did Margo say something she wouldn't take back? She sees her future as such a dismal thing—her life. Her life is this dismal thing. Damned. Cursed. She is afraid of living. But not death! Why? Why isn't she afraid of death?

One thing for sure, Tad was afraid of death. He liked his thoughts and his feelings; those thoughts and feelings were the only things he was certain he ever fully experienced. He couldn't remember the first thought or feeling he'd had as a baby, but he expected that there had to be one—some fixed sensation, whether in his crib, in his mother's womb, or as a spark in his father's eye, some fixed sensation was the very first, the genesis of it all. And if there was a first thought, it follows, there must be a last.

"Life is so unpredictable—it doesn't always deliver what you would expect, too many surprises. I've always feared that element of surprise. But, death, death is predictable. No surprises there! It's gonna happen, we're all sure of that, right? So, why keep playing the cards when you have a sure shot? I'll just fold and go straight to my big payout, thank you very much."

Predictable? She thinks death is predictable? Sure, maybe the fact of dying is—but nothing else about death is! No surprises?!?!

Tad so feared the cessation of thought and feeling, the possibility that death brought about the mind's end. But he didn't know for sure if it did—and that scared him. Whether or not thought and feeling ended with life's end was the surprise Tad figured death invited. After all, he knew what happened when he lived day by day, but he didn't know what would happen after he died.

How can she?

What if her most vital assumptions prove false—what if there is no heaven or hell? What if she, in fact, goes nowhere or becomes even more of the nothing she already thinks she is? What if, in those final moments, she learns that her existence had been nothing more than a fart in a vacuum, that there is no afterlife, that she does not get to see her family again?

She fears the element of surprise? Death might bring her a surprise and show her that her end is an utter end, not the new beginning she so craves.

Tad's mind was racing now—thoughts crowded with thoughts. He continually sketched out rudimentary rebuttals to each of her sentiments. But there were too many, and they came at him too fast. He felt jittery, antsy.

The messages in his head were inflamed by the messages from his body. His belly, empty of food, pooled with caffeinated water that worked to dehydrate him and pick at his nerves.

If he had a last nerve, which would get on it first—the caffeine or her words?

"See, I'm the one in control, here, Tad. And, the ultimate way for me to control my life is for me to end it. I won't let God or Mother Earth make this decision for me. I won't let God or Mother Earth decide when I'm to find death. The choice lies solely with me. I alone make that decision."

Tad pushed his glass away from his grasp. He'd had enough. He had a last nerve, and something was nearing it.

She'd been faced with what she ultimately considered a draw: to have the world end her or to have her end her self. And she romanticized the latter as a way to exert tenure and to escape the world's cruel design and sketch her own fate. She never once considered that, perchance, it had been by this very world's design that she would decide to leave at her own hand.

Power. Ownership. Hubris. All three, and little more, fused together in her head, allowing her to think her life was nothing but her own. Intrigue. Suspense. Like an anxious reader of a pulp novel, she wanted to flip to the final page and see how her story played out.

But not all stories end as one would expect.

~ 6 ~

They grew up only a few blocks away from each other, though they were complete strangers until further separated by four streets between two squares. When they lived on the same street, their paths never crossed; it wasn't until there was distance between them that they would meet.

Tad's father was a junior reverend at First Presbyterian Church—the Good Reverend Linders, as he came to be known, a proud husband, father, and spiritual leader seated in a lovely Second Square home.

Her family—her real family, that is—lived a few blocks away, closely after one of Second Square's corners, or distantly after Second Square's other three turns. As her parents were Catholics, the family didn't regularly see the Linderses and knew little more of them than the occasional pass-by.

This isn't to say that her folks were antisocial or maladapted to their Second Square home. It was just the way that things happened from time to time. Most people didn't know the mailman's name, didn't know what the neighbor's bathroom looked like or what went on behind locked, or unlocked, doors. It was simpler that way. And simply better. Especially in a town like this.

Elizabeth and Bernie—those were her parents' names. Bernie was a tall man who worked for the local newspaper— not as a journalist or a photographer or anything like that, but as a mailer. At this particular press, a "mailer"—though it might mean something else in some other place—was the glorified term for the person who saw to the distribution of the daily newspapers, counting the stacks and bundles and checking the distribution lists, things of that ilk. He'd had

this same job since two months after his high school gradua-
tion. Since the work and the paychecks were steady, he saw
no reason to seek out any type of "better" gig.

He met Elizabeth when she moved into the other half of
a Third Square duplex he came to call home. Elizabeth, fresh
out of graduate school, knocked on his door one afternoon to
see if she could enlist him, and any adequate tools he might
own, to help her hang her oversized diploma on the wall
above the television in her small living room. The degree
was for Elementary Education in the English Language, but
Chemistry seemed to dominate their initial interaction.

They hit it off immediately, and, in no time, they went
from living apart in one duplex to living together in one
home. Mere neighbors no more, Bernie turned in the keys to
his half of the duplex along with the key to his heart. They'd
each found the thing for which they'd both been blindly
searching for most of their lives—love.

Much to everyone's shock, and to some's dismay, they
were married a short six months after they'd first met. Their
marriage brought about some changes, though, for the new-
lywed couple, things seemed mainly the same.

During their brief courtship, Elizabeth had set aside her
career goals and focused primarily on her romantic ties to
Bernie. Rather than submitting résumés or attending semi-
nars, she packed picnic lunches and planned lovers' rendezvous. Her relationship with Bernie was what mattered most
to her. She wanted to be a good partner, a good friend.

And after their marriage, she wanted to be a good wife.
Bernie's salary, though not that impressive, was more than
enough to pay the bills and fund the fun. So Elizabeth put
her professional options on the back burner in pursuit of
marital bliss.

This was something that did not fare well with Elizabeth's older sister, Margo. Margo was a career woman

through and through—a lawyer, no less. Growing up, both girls learnt that a woman was free to do as a woman pleased. Woman's Liberation ushered in the ideal that a woman's place was wherever she wanted it to be, not in the home like centuries of patriarchs preached.

But Margo took this ideal to the extreme, believing that a woman's place was not in the home rather than not necessarily in the home. Margo's idea of liberation was not as full as her foremothers foresaw. It was still restricted, albeit in reverse. In Margo's skew, liberation, that cherished freedom every woman deserved, was limited—it meant that a woman had to work to be a free woman.

A woman who chose to be a housewife, or chose to be nothing more than a housewife, was not a liberated woman. Worse yet, the housewife damned the idea of liberation, feeding old stereotypes that the working woman worked to ruin. Freedom was freedom, if you made the right choice— or so Margo thought.

Margo didn't like Elizabeth's choice. And this strained their already strained relationship. The girls were sisters and little more. They had next to nothing in common. They'd both chosen different paths, and Margo refused to allow these paths to cross—Elizabeth's dirt road simply wasn't worthy of intersection with Margo's asphalt lane.

Whatever Margo felt about Elizabeth's choices, Elizabeth didn't herself feel. A woman could be whatever a woman wanted to be, and Elizabeth wanted to be a housewife and a homemaker. She enjoyed cooking meals for Bernie. Cleaning the house. Doing the laundry. Tending to the garden. She took pleasure in these things and was damn good at them. This was her calling, and she'd answered it with a smile.

Indeed, three years into her household career, her hard work paid off—with a well-deserved promotion.

Her promotion was from wife to mother, and it came with

great benefits. The first little joy to crawl out of Elizabeth's vagina was a baby girl named Joyce. Joyce was born with a broken collar bone, and they spent the next three and a half years coddling her until they had another daughter. *Her*. At 27 inches long, weighing 11.5 pounds, she was a big baby. Maybe that's how and why Joyce broke her collar bone when Elizabeth birthed her, widening the path for her baby sister?

One half of a duplex on Third Square seemed too small for a family of four, so Bernie's widowered father opened the door of his Second Square home to his son's family. Bernie's father, Frank, was in his tarnished golden years and needed both the companionship of the family and the daily assistance Elizabeth provided. Bernie, Elizabeth, and the girls got a bigger roof over their heads while Frank got hot meals, clean rooms, and the warmth of other bodies and voices floating his halls.

The five of them lived together, as a narrowly extended family, for nearly four years until Frank passed away in his sleep one afternoon while Elizabeth simmered homemade spaghetti sauce on the stove one floor below. Bernie inherited the house from his father and managed to maintain a similar living standard through the considerable amount of money Frank left him in addition to the overtime shifts he took on at the paper.

What fuel for Margo's fire! They'd inherited something they hadn't earned—so, naturally, they didn't deserve this lifestyle.

Margo'd worked for everything she had. She went to law school for three years, studied her ass off, put her nose to the grind. She worked on course outlines, sucked up to professors (quite literally, though she wouldn't admit it), and volunteered as both a school tour guide and a tutor for foreign students who couldn't comprehend linguistic dissimilarities in American law.

Margo tugged at the rope ladder and did the impossible—she made her way up. She'd married a man who otherwise outclassed her, one who had both a job with, and old money from, his grandfather's insurance company. David, who she'd bagged twelve years earlier while working an internship in Town Hall during the summer between her second and third years of law school. David, who decided to buy the cow since he definitely wasn't getting the milk for free. She changed her religion for him. Changed her hairstyle, her last name.

Everything that Margo had ever done in her life, she'd done to get to this point—to get what she deserved. She earned it all. When Bernie and Elizabeth, and those two fat little babies, had something fall in their laps, Margo was enraged. What was once distance between her and her sister became bitterness.

When Margo looked at Elizabeth and Bernie, she saw two lazy good-for-nothings who lost ambition far before they found luck. But more so than she resented the couple, she resented their children, her nieces in blood.

Margo felt sick to her stomach when she saw the little tots run around a large house they didn't deserve. The toys and games were bought with money they shouldn't have ever seen. Even the haircuts on their tiny heads blighted Margo—the scissors used to trim their soft manes, and the scissors alone, should have been more than their good-for-nothing housewife mommy could ever afford!

When Margo came around to visit the family, which wasn't often at all, she was cold and stern. She'd scoff at any mess around the house and ignore her nieces' efforts to show her affection or involve her in play. She'd perch like a flower surrounded by thorns, stemmed away from contact in a frosty dewed winter bloom.

Margo wore her bitterness and resentment on her sleeve.

Sure, the kids were too young to see it, thank God. But Elizabeth and Bernie weren't. They could see, and sense, it each time Margo came around. But they kept thinking, hoping, that maybe, just maybe, things would change. Margo was the only immediate family Elizabeth had left, and Bernie had no siblings. Margo was all the girls would ever know as family other than their parents—and Elizabeth and Bernie saw that as a tattered thread worth keeping, though in desperate need of repair.

But, rest assured, neither Margo nor her thinly veiled torment really impacted the family's daily lives. Maybe Margo would be there for a couple of hours one day a month. Every other hour of every other day of that month was met with more ease and cheer; Elizabeth worked to ensure that.

Elizabeth, the homemaker, strived to make her home a wonderful place for her children as they grew up. Their home was not only clean and safe, not to mention vibrantly decorated, but also magical, mystical, at times. It was a land of fairytales, both the ones Elizabeth read to her daughters and the ones they played out in the skits they performed in their basement.

The meals were hearty. There were rubber duckies in the bathtub and drawings on the refrigerator. Midnight snacks, from time to time, and little plastic swimming pools in the backyard.

Lots of movies, sometimes theater shows, other times drive-in shows, still other times at home plopped on the couch. The girls were fascinated by movies. Of course, they viewed mostly cartoons and other stories made for children—though, occasionally, flicks such as "Jaws" made it into the line-up (which gave way to Joyce's fascination with sharks as she felt sorry for the film's underwater antagonist).

Joyce tended to like the more realistic movies, while her younger sister far better enjoyed the fairytales with happy endings. Indeed, "Snow White" was her favorite movie in her youngest years. She loved it so much that Bernie took on the practice of serenading her each night before she went to bed, belting out "Someday your prince will come" and other adaptations of the film's second most famous song's lyrics.

Enough already, right?

Not yet. Their childhood together was one of those ideal ones you never hear about, a pleasant account that makes you gag and question how much sugary hindsight came to coat it. But that's how it was. A childhood is either good or bad, and it just so happens that theirs was the former.

Sure, they had some "hard times"—where "hard" is defined as little kids define it. "Hard," like the time the girls ate a pint of raw sauerkraut ball batter and got sick off of it. That sure ruined their taste for sauerkraut balls! "Hard," like the times they'd get in trouble for ignoring their pet poodle Mollie's call from nature and allow her to go potty on the carpet. "Hard," like how they got scolded when they'd try to hide Mollie's accident from their parents by picking up her poop and matting it in a dirty sock.

But the "hard times" were not really that special. What was that special, for them, were the other times, like the little parties Elizabeth would organize for their birthdays or at appropriate holiday and seasonal times.

Around Christmas one year, Elizabeth threw such a party, coining it a birthday party for Jesus, and invited all the young girls from the neighborhood. With her daughters, she baked two dozen chocolate cupcakes and one small chocolate cake, on which she wrote "Happy Birthday Jesus." As the time for the party drew near, that special little cake was nowhere to be found.

Elizabeth's younger daughter stepped up to find it. With magnifying glass in hand, like the Holy Ghost, she searched the house until she found the empty cake pan underneath an antique potty chair in the upstairs bathroom—precisely where she'd hidden it right after she'd snuck Jesus' birthday cake away and eaten it. Elizabeth wasn't mad though—after all, it was quite funny; it's not every day that a child gets the chance to rob Christ. *Margo would be proud—such a shame she wasn't invited to the party!*

Of course, it couldn't all be fun and games—after all, the girls had to go to school at some point, right? But, even this, Elizabeth worked to make pleasurable for her children.

In addition to the praise she gave them for their successes, the consolation she gave them for their failures, and the attention she gave to their efforts, she offered them encouragement.

By the time both the girls were in school, Elizabeth would regularly put simple little notes in their lunches or hidden in their backpacks, reassurances and reminders mixed with inspirational messages. As the girls got older, the notes got longer, assuredly containing large words that Elizabeth knew her daughters would likely not be able to read or understand, giving them a reason to learn a word's pronunciation and meaning.

When Elizabeth's younger daughter was 11 years old, she taped a note to the bathroom mirror for her baby girl to read:

Hey Princess!

Look in the mirror, and what do you see?
Your face smiling back as you read this note from me.
Your blue eyes look shiny and bright.
It appears you've had a restful night.
I bet your dreams are shelved, and reality has set in.
Soon collect all your thoughts, and let your day begin.

I have a feeling your day will be a success.
So go on girl, and start to get dressed.
The bus is coming; the book bag is packed laying on the chair.
Oops, better give a last brush to your hair.
And just like it's happened hundreds of times before
Mollie starts barking and chasing as you go out the door.
You yell, "I love you mom," and I reply, "Me too, have a nice day."
You're going to school; what more can I say?
Oh yes, I have one thing to say, so pay heed –
Perhaps it's the only advice you'll ever need.
Put your best effort forward, and do your best
Whether it's playing a sport, giving an opinion, or taking a test.
If you sincerely do the best you can possibly do,
I can be proud of you, and you can be proud of you too.

Love,
Momma

Her daughter took the note to school with her and read it over and over again, fascinated by the rhyme and focusing on some of those big words she knew Momma would later explain to her. Little did she know, as she sat there during lunch period, flecking the note with drops of ketchup and crinkling it in her grasp, that, when she got home, Momma wouldn't be there to explain those words. Little did she know that this was her last note from Momma.

Elizabeth had been a life-long diabetic. And now she was a dead diabetic. She went into diabetic shock that afternoon, when no one else was home—when Bernie found her, she was still alive though already dead. Elizabeth was rushed to the hospital, where Bernie learnt that she was brain dead. He made the difficult decision to pull her off of life-support and watched as her chest heaved one last time.

When the girls arrived home from school, they were met by Margo and David. They were ushered into the house and sent to do their homework without explanation. Some time later, Bernie called his home, to speak with his wife's sister, minutes after Elizabeth expired. He asked her not to tell his daughters, claiming that task as a father's duty.

Though Margo agreed, she did not oblige. She called the girls down and frankly told them that their mother was dead, later justifying her actions as a mental lapse due to the gravity of the situation.

The girls were heartbroken at the loss of their mother, to say the least. For the two of them, the funeral was a blur of confusion and pain. There were so many people at the funeral home. So many old ladies that smelled like cheap perfume. So many men and women hugging and kissing them or patting their heads. And then there was Momma—lying there, dressed up and made up, not moving. *Dead.*

But it was what followed the funeral that caused the girls the greatest pain. The time without Momma was practically unbearable. Sometimes, one or the other of them would wake up in the middle of the night and shout out for Momma and then sob when she remembered that Momma wasn't there.

Bernie grieved too, of course, but he put up his best front to make things easier on the girls. He still took them to movies. He tried to cook some of Elizabeth's recipes, tried to write them notes. But he lacked the same flare.

Around ten months after Momma's death, just when things were getting as close to normal as anyone could expect things to be, right after Bernie had tried to infuse the otherwise dark summer with hours of sunshine at a local pool, Joyce complained that her back hurt. Bernie shrugged it off at first, thinking she must have had sunburn.

But Joyce complained about these pains again two days later. She looked awfully pale and kept vomiting throughout the day. Bernie took her to the emergency room, where he fell over onto a tray of medical supplies when the doctor informed him that Joyce had to be moved to the intensive care unit because she was having an acute pancreatic attack.

Like the saying goes, it was an acute attack, but there was nothing cute about it. Joyce was diagnosed with Pancreatitis—a disease which most normally affects older, life-long alcoholic males, with none of the above even remotely describing Joyce. Fifteen years old. Female. Never drank a sip of booze, other than during the sacrament at weekly masses. Perhaps she would have been better off eating Jesus' birthday cake, like her younger sister, rather than drinking his blood.

Joyce was very bad off. She was on so much pain medication that she couldn't communicate intelligibly. She'd drift in and out of coherency as her condition worsened. Her triglyceride levels were off the roof. Her blood glucose level was insane. Her kidneys were failing. She was dying.

Bernie spent as much time as he could at the hospital with Joyce, though he didn't forget he had another daughter. He tried to keep her away from the horrible visuals at the hospital, but he couldn't continually deny her the chance to see her fading sister.

"Are you scared JJ?"

That's what she called her. Her sister. She called her "JJ," since her middle name was June.

"JJ, can you hear me? Are you scared?"

"I'm not scared. I saw Momma. Momma said I'd be okay."

"You saw Momma? Where is she? Where is she, JJ?"

"She's right here. Momma's right here. I can see her…

Can you?"

She looked around the room in search of Momma. She tried so hard to see Momma like Joyce did. She saw Bernie biting his lip. She saw Joyce, her JJ, opening and closing her eyes and trying to move. She did not see Momma. But Joyce said she was there—so Momma must be there. If only she could see her!

Later that night, once Bernie collected his surprisingly cheered younger daughter and went home, he received a call from the hospital informing him that Joyce had slipped into a coma. An impossible 19 hours later, Bernie held his lifeless first daughter in his arms as he pleaded with God for an explanation.

"JJ's with Momma now," that's what he told her.

And she replied, "I know. JJ told me. She told me that she saw Momma, but I didn't see her… Will I ever get to see Momma or JJ again, Papa?"

"Yes. Yes you will. We'll all meet up in heaven someday, and it'll be just like it always was."

"I sure hope so!"

The thing about seeds is that they plant so easily in fresh soil.

Fifteen months later, Bernie had a stroke and brain aneurysm shortly after dropping his 13-year-old daughter off at school for an evening choir practice. He died on the operating table where the surgeons tried to patch an aneurysm the size of a plum—something they marveled at, for sure, since the average brain aneurysm is the size of a pea.

It was at this point that Margo and David stepped in to take the reins. They scooped up what was left of the now defunct family unit and took her to their home where she spent the immediately following days practicing her singing on the bed in the upstairs spare room.

When Margo asked her why she was singing, she informed Margo that she was practicing the song she wanted to sing at Papa's funeral. "Someday your prince will come," she bellowed, before Margo insisted, "Stop that nonsense! You will NOT sing THAT in a church!"

"But, Aunt Margo, Papa used to sing it to me every night before I went to sleep. Now, I want to sing it for him before he goes to sleep forever."

"You'll do no such thing, young lady! Have you no sense of pride? No sense at all? You're definitely your mother's daughter."

With that, her idea was tabled, and Margo arranged your average respectful, run-of-the-mill funeral services for Bernie.

And that's how she came to board with Margo and David in their First Square home. Margo, the public defender, and David, the insurance man—poor replacements for her parents; they were both thin, gaunt, and now they had a pudgy little teenager to care for. They had no idea how to take care of a child—and that was obvious.

Everything was obvious in those first couple of years. Obvious both to Margo and David and to her—obvious how truly out of place she was.

This place, Margo's and David's house—it was something altogether different. But she got used to it, sort of—she figured she'd leave one day, even though it's been thirteen years and she still hasn't. *Still hasn't—yet…*

Margo and David were Presbyterian—well, Margo converted to Presbyterianism when she married David—and it was through this affiliation that she got entwined with the Linderses.

The Linderses had only one child, our dear Tad. Mrs. Linders worked as a nurse at the hospital for most of her adult life, though after her son was born she drastically cut her work hours down and took on a desk job in the hospital's administrative offices in order to tend to her young boy during his most formative years. *Both a liberated woman and a mother!*

When her little Tad turned 10 years old, Mrs. Linders decided she wanted to enter the full-time workforce once more and took her nursing boards again to get recertified so that she could, professionally, be all that she had once been.

The Linderses, quite familiar with Margo and David as avid church-goers, inquired as to whether their lovely 15-year-old niece would be interested in babysitting Tad on those occasions when Mrs. Linders' work schedule overlapped with the Good Reverend's office hours at the church. Eager to please the Linderses, Margo and David agreed without hesitation, and without actually consulting their niece.

When she learnt of her new assignment, she was infuriated. After all, she was a young girl, a teenager. She wanted to hang out with boys and gossip with other girls. She wanted to have fun. What fun could she have sitting with a 10-year-old boy—in a holy man's house, no less!

Despite her objection, she took on the charge, all the while loathing the little brat who occupied her time when she should've been out with her friends. He ate too much. He watched too much television. He was messy, greedy, and sneaky. And he had his hand down his pants a lot.

Her role as babysitter didn't last long though. Within the year, shortly before the Good Reverend passed away, she was replaced by Mrs. Ballow, an 80-year-old lonesome widow who lived two streets away from the Linderses.

Indeed, it was a bad year, the crown jewel of too many.

~ 7 ~

"And, that decision has been made—all I'm willing to give is one more day. I'm doing it tomorrow evening… You know, you have to be there with me. I want you there."

There with her? To watch her die? No. I wish I were blind. So that I wouldn't have to see it.

I don't want to be there and watch death. I've seen dead, but never dying. Never fleeing, escaping. Could I even comprehend it?

No. I do not want this. But she does.

So I must be there. Alice, lend me your blind eyes!

"Well, I guess that brings us right back to where we started, huh Tad? Right back to the beginning, to my question—how I asked you to help me. My baptism, my cleansing. I need you to do it… So, what do you say?"

As usual, Tad said nothing. But that nothing was not his reply—his silence was not a refusal.

His face was tingling. His cheeks felt hard and expanding. He glanced down at the table and watched her fuss with her soft-pack of cigarettes. *Her wrists are so small.* His eyes were lifted up to meet hers, carried open to full watch by the painstakingly unhurried lifting of his heavy eyelids. His eyes felt full, swelling, and warm—his vision seemed to improve.

The first drop of holy water he was to spill for her slowly wept from his right eye. He raised his jaw and upper lip to speak, the muscle contractions squeezing out a tear from his other eye, but swiftly bit his mouth shut and jerked his head upward to look at the dangling lamp above their table.

He quickly sniffled before looking at her again. His eyes were more relaxed now, still glistening with a saline sheen.

85

He stared straight at her, breathing heavily through his mouth the whole while and rarely ever blinking.

Their gaze was locked.

"Pam," she called out, "can you bring me a glass of water? No ice, no straw. Just water. A big glass of water. Lukewarm."

Yes, she chose water. I knew she would.

~ 8 ~

In the beginning, God created the Heaven and the Earth—but, lest you forget, before there was light, there was water.

In that beginning, the Earth was without form. Void. Darkness covered the face of the deep. Yet, something moved. The Spirit of God. It moved upon the face of the waters.

And God looked out into the watery abyss, the saturated apocalypse waiting to happen, and said, "Let there be light." And there was light.

God saw the light. It was damn good. And God divided the light from the darkness. The evening from the dawn.

And so went the First Day.

But God didn't stop there. He looked out over the waters and said, "Let there be a firmament in the midst of the waters, and let it divide the waters from the waters."

Thus God made the skies and called the waters above them Heaven.

And so went the Second Day.

God looked down on the Earth, as he still does today, and said, "Let the waters under the heaven be gathered together unto one place, and let the dry land appear." And God called the dry land Earth. The gathering together of the lower waters, he called the Seas.

God looked at what he had created. He was pleased. It was good.

And so went the Third Day.

God said, "Let there be lights in the firmament of the

heaven to divide the day from the night; and let them be for signs, and for seasons, and for days, and years." And God made two great lights—a greater light to rule the day, and a lesser light to rule the night. He set the stars in the sky, to punctuate the night's thick mystique.

And, oh yes, God saw it and thought, knew, that it was good.

And so went the Fourth Day.

God looked to the Earth again and called for life, "Let the waters bring forth abundantly the moving creature that hath life, and fowl that may fly above the earth in the open firmament of heaven." And God created the whales and the fish, and the birds that flew in the skies.

Yes, sure enough, his first brood sprouted from the waters.

God saw that it was good and blessed his first-born creatures, "Be fruitful, and multiply."

And so went the Fifth Day.

God turned to the Earth's dry surface and said, "Let the earth bring forth the living creature after his kind." And it was so.

"Let us make man in our image, after our likeness: and let them have dominion over the fish of the sea, and over the fowl of the air, and. . . over every creeping thing that creepeth upon the earth." And God created man in his own image. In the image of God, he created man and woman.

God blessed them and said, "Be fruitful, and multiply, and replenish the earth, and subdue it: and have dominion over the fish of the sea, and over the fowl of the air, and over every living thing that moveth upon the earth."

And God said, "Behold, I have given you every herb bearing seed . . . and every tree . . . for meat." Thus God gave man and woman many good things to gobble.

God took in the totality of his creation. He saw that it was good and decided to rest.

Exhausted, he looked down (up)on man and woman and muttered, 'I've done this all for you… But, I'm so damn tired now—I need a break from all this shit.'

And so went the Sixth Day.

Tomorrow will be the Seventh—she'll slip away when God's not looking.

Within moments that dragged on like shapeless ages, Pam appeared at their table with a yellow frosted 20-ounce plastic tumbler nearly filled to the top with tap water. She held the glass in her left hand and placed her right hand on her hip to inquire, "You kids 'bout ready for your check yet? You been here for like five hours."

Pam wasn't entirely accurate. In fact, they'd only been there for about four and a half hours or so. It was just before midnight. Pam's shift was to end in nine minutes, and she wanted to make sure that her customers paid before then so that she could get what tips were coming to her.

"Oh, yeah, Pam, sure. Thanks… Here, just take this and keep the change," she handed Pam a $10 bill, more than enough to pay for her and Tad's beverages with plenty left over for Pam's tip.

She had a tendency to over tip waiters and waitresses. She felt obligated to do so in certain situations—situations such as this, where she occupied a great deal of time and space such that 15 to 20 percent of a few dollars was too close to nothing to be comfortable. She also tended to over tip bartenders—in large part because she felt they deserved it as a lifeline for the debauchery and dredging they dealt with daily, but in even larger part because she truly envied them for some unknown yet particular reason.

Like a hungry seagull diving to the shallowest regions of

the ocean, Pam's right hand swooped through the air to catch the money, "Thanks, 'hun. You kids take it easy. Stay outta trouble, right?"

"Oh, I'll try, Pam. Believe me, I will try," she chuckled as Pam placed the tumbler of water down on the table.

But these were the generations of the Heavens and of the Earth when they were created, not when they were. These were the days that God made them, before the plants had yet been rooted or the herbs began to grow, before God had caused it to rain upon the Earth or put man there to till the ground.

God sent a gift to the Earth. A mist of water. Water, to feed the whole face of the ground. Then, from the soil of the Earth, that very soil made muddy by the rain, God formed man and breathed the breath of life into his nostrils. Thus man became a living soul.

God planted a Garden, a nice one, east in Eden. God planted trees in the ground, both pretty ones that were pleasing to look at and nourishing ones that bore fruit. Amidst the trees, he placed two at the center of the Garden—the tree of life and the tree of knowledge of good and evil.

A river was set out of Eden to water the Garden. From thence it was parted, in each of four directions.

And God put the man he had created into the Garden of Eden to dress it and to keep it. God commanded unto the man, "Of every tree of the garden thou mayest freely eat: But of the tree of the knowledge of good and evil, thou shalt not eat of it: for in the day that thou eatest thereof thou shalt surely die."

God saw that the man walked the Earth alone and decided to make for him a suitable companion. And out of the ground God formed the beast of the field and the fowl of the air. He brought them to Adam for Adam to name.

And Adam named all the animals. But Adam was still alone.

God caused Adam to fall into a deep sleep. As he slept God ripped out one of Adam's ribs and made from that rib a woman and brought her unto man. And Adam said, "This is now bone of my bones, and flesh of my flesh: she shall be called Woman, because she was taken out of Man."

And so, for the first time, woman received man's bone. For the first time, man and woman cleaved—together, one flesh.

They were both naked, the man and his wife, and were not ashamed. Not even as they fucked.

The tumbler of water sat between them, somewhere closer to her than to Tad. She leant forward a little and inched it over to his side of the table. She gave him a coy grin before she crossed her arms in front of her chest and playfully nodded.

He looked down at the water. It was perfectly still. Quite calm. No ice, no straw. *Just like she had ordered.*

He extended his right arm forward and brought his hand to contact the tumbler. He felt the pocks of the tumbler's frosting.

He ran his index and middle fingers up and down the height of the glass as he thought over what he was about to do.

If there was any chance of getting out of this, the time was upon him. He could get up and walk out of Larry's, and that would be that. He could end his involvement with her ridiculous plan.

But, of course, he didn't. He couldn't.

His fingers reached the rim of the glass. He dipped them into the water and rolled the tiny molecules of her impending salvation between his fingertips and thumb. It was neither cold nor hot. *Lukewarm.*

Now, the serpent was the most cunning of any beast God had created. And the serpent said unto the woman, "Hath God said, 'Ye shall not eat of every tree of the garden'?"

And the woman said unto the serpent, "We may eat of the fruit of the trees of the garden: But of the fruit of the tree which is in the midst of the garden, God hath said, 'Ye shall not eat of it, neither shall ye touch it, lest ye die.'"

The serpent crawled closer to the woman and spat, "Ye shall not surely die: For God doth know that in the day ye eat thereof, then your eyes shall be opened, and ye shall be as gods, knowing good and evil."

The woman looked at the tree and saw that it was awfully pretty, with plump fruits of wisdom dangling from its branches. She plucked a ripe bud. And she did eat of that fruit, and gave it also unto her husband who did eat as well.

And the eyes of them both were opened. Opened wide. *Big eyes. Like quarters.* They looked at themselves and at each other and knew that they were naked. And they sewed fig leaves together to make aprons to cover their bodies.

They heard the voice of God in the Garden and hid themselves amongst the trees. And God called unto Adam, "Where art thou?"

Adam said unto God, "I heard thy voice in the garden, and I was afraid, because I was naked; and I hid myself."

And God said, "Who told thee that thou wast naked? Hast thou eaten of the tree . . . ?"

"The woman whom thou gavest to be with me, she gave me of the tree, and I did eat."

And God said unto the woman, "What is this that thou hast done?"

And the woman said, "The serpent beguiled me, and I did eat."

Indeed, the man and the woman both did succumb, one to the serpent and one to his sleeve.

So God took from the serpent its legs and cast Adam and Eve out of the Garden of Eden, covered in sacks filled with a stuffing of three parts Shame and two parts Original Sin.

"I'm ready when you are, Tad."

Tad clasped the tumbler between both his hands. He held it tightly. His hands were trembling, shaking, on fire. Could he melt the cheap plastic?

He let go of the tumbler and began to lift his body out of the booth. His knees felt like they would cave on him, but nonetheless he persisted until he was standing tall beside her at the table. Once sitting parallel to each other, she now sat perpendicular to Tad's towering frame.

She turned her head to look up at him. Her neck created a lovely arch as she took both hands and tousled her hair lightly so that it was no longer tucked behind her ears. She closed her eyes for a moment while her dimpled cheeks pressed to the waters above, up to heaven, to reveal the most cheeky, teethy, and entirely fulfilled smile.

She opened her eyes even wider—*big eyes, like quarters*—and strained them to look at and above Tad without further fixing her posture.

His right arm reached forward to the table and grabbed the tumbler of lukewarm water. He raised it to his chest, held it there for a moment, and then steered it nearer to her head.

She quietly, almost inaudibly, gasped and looked up at it him with wanton eyes.

Tad tilted the tumbler slightly, allowing a slow stream of water to trickle down. It first hit the crown of her head and almost disappeared into her dark hair.

He tilted the tumbler further to give the water, *and her*, a greater rush.

Now, ounces, rather than mere drops, of water doused her head. Her hair looked lacquered. Streams found their ways to her forehand, her shoulders, her clothes.

Her eyes remained opened as Tad poured. Open eyes, fixed on him, with water running down her brows and through her lashes. Open eyes, opened wide, fixed on him.

Her breath was heavy and hard. She opened her mouth. And, pink cell by pink cell, she let her tongue out from within. For the first time since the start of her baptism, and only for a few seconds, she closed her eyes as she lapped at that water collecting near her tongue.

Oh, to taste her water!

The tumbler was empty—the water, all gone. Tad shook out every last drop and then threw it to the floor. Cheap plastic glasses never break when they hit cheap linoleum flooring. This was no exception.

But they do make loud noises when they land. And it was this that drew Larry's' workers' and patrons' attention.

No one had noticed when Tad stood up. No one had heard her quiet gasp. No one even noticed when Tad poured the water over her head. But they heard the tumbler tumble to the ground. And then, they saw it.

They saw her. Wet and sitting there. Smiling and soaked. And Tad. Standing beside the table. Flustered. Shaking.

Things got a little louder and a lot more chaotic at that point.

Pam ran over to the table, "You guys better get the hell outta here. Right now. I don't know what your problem is. But, get out. Now!"

The folks at Larry's sure got their money's worth tonight. Heads turned. Customers whispered and gawked. Barlow and Tom-Tom, the short order cooks, came out of the kitchen to see what had happened. Condescending tones all around.

But one voice sounded different. One voice stood out in the crowd. Someone was laughing.

It was Alice. Alice Worth.

Had she seen *what I just did?*

~ 9 ~

Together, they left Larry's and walked the usual route home. Still drenched from her recent rebirth, she practically skipped along the sidewalk. Grinning, overjoyed, she was ready for death.

Tad walked with a bowed head, inspecting each drop of water that trailed her path. *Dark spots on the concrete. Her legacy.*

"So, tomorrow night, around 7:00—that feels right to me. You will be there with me, right? … You have to. So, be there. Come around 7:00… Yeah, 7:00… This means so much to me, Tad. I won't forget it—ever. "

And neither will I.

They parted ways at Second Square, to find their own separate ways to their own separate houses. He was amazed, and scared, by how gracefully she strolled away.

Once in her room, she shut the door and immediately took a double dose of prescription sleeping pills so that she could spend the night, and most of the next day, outside of the waking hours in which she might commit some sin.

Tad, on the other hand, found no rest. He spent his time thinking about what he would do in her wake. He thought about his future, framing it in terms from the past.

You see, after the Good Reverend passed, Mrs. Linders endured a stint of grave depression which would culminate in the late evening hours after Tad went to bed and she realized the utter solitude surrounding her. Mrs. Linders, or Sophie, as the adult, grown-up, and mature population called her, eventually forgot whatever misgivings her late husband might have had and spent these hours pining over her loss of companionship, duty, and, for lack of a more appropriate word in her vocabulary, consortium.

To quash the strongest pangs of her depression, she'd spend hours seated in the Reverend's recliner—there, perched and viewing hour upon hour of late night television. The first television character to spike her interest was a November-aged televangelist who promised her, and the rest of his faithful viewers, a life filled with happiness, forgiveness, and opportunity—for a small donation, of course.

Though she didn't precisely know from which secular pulpit Dob Barley, her beloved televangelist, delivered his truths, she could not get enough of him and his TV antics. Each night Dob did nothing short of turning water into wine in Sophie's eyes. His miraculous healings. His spiritual forecasts. This man was the real thing—or at least he had to be since the real thing was gone.

On those nights when she had to work the late shift at the hospital, she would record Dob's programs on her trusty VCR and play them ad nauseam during the daytime hours which otherwise would never've been graced with such programming. She memorized many of his inspirational sayings and would chant along with Dob as he lead his mass for the masses.

Eventually, Sophie, Mrs. Sophie Linders, the late Reverend's wife, decided to put her money where her mouth was and phone in her support. And she did so on more than one occasion, always delighted to receive a small token of appreciation from the religious headquarters of Dob Barley. The little gifts were mostly pins and bookmarks wearing little slogans Sophie never quite understood, with phrases like "Redemption—You Won't Find IT in a Song" and "Who Needs Three Birds When You've Got Twelve Apostles?"

These things soon scattered the house, often finding their ways aside the teacup of the occasional visitor or pinned to

Tad's backpack. It came to look as if Sophie was running a local field office for Dob Barley's cult. She was like a woman obsessed, though she would have never realized or admitted that since obsession seemed outside the realm of the perfect world Dob and his trinkets helped her build in her mind and impose on her home.

This world, however, was soon to crumble. There'd be another ghost to haunt the Linders estate.

With a thermos of herbal mint tea in hand and a plate of low-sugar peanut butter cookies awaiting her on the side table flanking the late Reverend's chair, Sophie entered her living room one night to conduct her tele-worship routine as usual. To her surprise, when she flicked on her familiar channel 18, her dear Dob was not there. She checked her watch—was it not 1:30 a.m.? She checked the remote, changed the batteries, manually shifted back and forth to channel 18. She could not find Dob.

She rushed to check the TV listings, where Dob's name was nowhere to be found. Scared, angered, and annoyed, she called her local cable company—and, much to her disbelief and dismay, she learnt that Dob's show was cancelled from channel 18's lineup and that, to the best of the cable company's knowledge, Dob's program was not picked up by any other station.

Over the next few weeks, she spent her late night hours buried in futile attempts at writing letters to broadcast companies and starting local and national petitions which never made it past her front door. As a final resort, she called Dob Barley's headquarters—only to find out that Dob had passed away in a fatal car crash of "undisclosed" origins. Yes, poor Sophie, Dob died.

Sophie, Mrs. Sophie Linders, the late Reverend's wife, Dob Barley's abandoned fledgling, felt loss, and lost, all over again. It was as if the good Reverend had died again. Two men of God, gone. Two men of God, dead.

In fact, hadn't God given her these men? And wasn't it God who took them away from her? What God would do that? What God could do that?

Men of God. Men for God. Men from God. Gone. Taken away. She'd given her life to the Reverend, been a good wife, gave him a son. When she lost him, she'd given her life to Dob, been a good follower, given him her time, her energy, her money.

Gone. Both of them. Gone.

Empty again, she needed to be filled. She needed a new man—and she needed a new God.

Enter Puss.

Dob Barley's late night show was replaced with a set of infomercials by the MetGo company that continually looped throughout the late night television hours. With nothing better to do with her time, having lost anything to look forward to, or to look at, Sophie tuned in to the nightly MetGo infomercials.

One night, while staring at one of Dob's bookmarks as a MetGo infomercial clattered on in the background, Sophie made her first call to the MetGo Shopping telephone lines—to order an amazing home-brewing product that, with the right ingredients, could turn water into beer. She spoke with a pleasant man named Rob who helped her complete her order and offered her a free month's supply of yeast!

Only three nights later, Sophie found herself talking to Rob again, this time to order an incredible set of oils from which one could craft his or her own personal perfume scent. Less than a week later, she spoke to Rob again, ordering a set of kitchen knives never in need of sharpening.

It wasn't until the fourth time that Sophie spoke with Rob that he took the conversation to a different level.

He commented that he was glad to hear her voice again, since he felt like he and Sophie were old friends, as they'd spoken a few times before, and since he thought her voice was sexy. Next, came the questions—if she was single, what she looked like, what she was wearing.

At first, Sophie was a little set back—but, in no time, she disclosed more than enough personal information to have Rob suggest that they meet. As it turned out, Rob worked for MetGo out of his home—a home, interestingly enough, only about a two-hour drive from Sophie's address, which Rob knew quite well by now from the orders Sophie'd placed.

Rob was willing to drive to meet Sophie, and Sophie was willing to host. They arranged to meet the very next day, at high noon, while Tad was still in school.

After hours of primping, Sophie sat patiently at the kitchen table. Then, the doorbell rang. She sprinted to the door, where she found an awkwardly attractive man about ten years her junior. He was cleverly dressed in a white button-down shirt and snug blue jeans, adorning thick plastic black eyeglasses.

"Rob?" she asked.

"Of course. Though, all my friends call me Puss," replied the young man.

"Puss? Why?"

"Well, ya' know," he began, as he motioned toward his hairline, "my hair. They say it looks like cat ears."

Sophie tried to inconspicuously take a gander. His hairline receded slightly on both sides of his forehead, to pointy peaks on his skull. His hair was jet black and short but spiked up all along his forehead and crown. Sure, sure, the resemblance was there, even if slight. Sure, sure, he looked like a cat. A pussy cat. Puss!

"Well then, Puss, it's nice to meet you."

"And, it's nice to finally meet you… Sophie."

With that, Rob, err Puss, entered the Linders home—and, contrary to what we might assume about Sophie herself, he soon thereafter entered the Linders widow as well.

It was your average whirlwind courtship after that. Puss drove in for afternoon delights at least once a week for the next three months, though Sophie, of course, owing concern to a now 12-year-old Tad, never ventured out to Puss's neck of the woods.

Sophie no longer needed to shop from the late Reverend's recliner. Her late night trysts with television infomercials turned into late night thoughts of Puss, or conversations with him on the phone.

Eventually, both lovers grew frustrated with the distance and its import into their affair. So much time apart, so much distance—something needed to be done. With the flicker of his long lashes, Puss came up with a solution. He suggested that he move in with Sophie and child, to take this romance to the next level.

Sophie, who, by now, had found a new God in the man who now filled her, quickly agreed. Without any prior warning, Tad came home from school one day to find two suitcases and four boxes in the living room and an unfamiliar man parked on the floor in front of the television, watching a show demonstrating the finer points of taking a modern spin on a traditional pot roast with red russet potatoes and thin sticks of carrots. *Oh, the red wine reduction did sound appealing!*

Tad looked, at first, in disbelief, until his mother ran into the room and gleefully shouted, "Oh, Tad! Meet Puss! The new man of the house—he'll take care of us both!"

Tad nodded his head and went to the kitchen.

Over the next two weeks, the products Sophie had ordered from MetGo arrived. Puss took Sophie and Tad out to dinner on the small commission he'd made from the sales. Sophie never even used the items, giggling as she repeatedly proclaimed that she'd found something better to do with her time.

Tad never really paid Puss any mind. Nor did Puss pay Tad any mind. To each, the other was merely there, something to keep Sophie occupied and happy. Sometimes Puss would try to talk to Tad or to engage Tad in his life. But Tad never really cared to entertain the entertainment.

Despite their lack of communication though, Puss was never judgmental of, or cruel to, Tad. He just went about his days, caring only about himself and, at times, Sophie.

Indeed, Puss proved to be somewhat of a loaf. Once he moved in with Sophie and Tad, he gave up his astute career with MetGo and spent most of his time watching television and painting the basement walls. Within the first six months that he lived there, the walls went from their original white to a canary yellow to a baby blue to a lime green and finally to a brick red. Sophie, who paid for the many layers of paint with which Puss colored, was amused by what she considered Puss's cleverness and attention to detail.

In those first six months, Puss shared a lot of personal details with Sophie, as one would expect. And what a storied past he had!

At 30 years old, he had only been in the United States for eleven years. Before that, he reported, he was a native of Ireland, where he had some dealings in the IRA since his late pre-teen years. Due to the fact that he was involved in a well-publicized car bombing, he fled the country at 19 years old so as to escape the national security hunting him down.

Once in America, he took on a nom de plume, Rob Robertson, in an attempt to escape the manhunt for Patrick "Puss" McClantry. His jet black hair, as well as his Lynyrd

Skynyrd tattoo, was part of his new identity.

This information, as he stressed to Sophie, was to remain entirely between the two of them—though it was Puss himself who let it slip many a time whilst drunk and conversing with some other random drunkard at Larry's.

For four years, Puss slept loosely under his cover, wrapped in Sophie's arms and monies and nestled in the inconsequential friendships he developed at Larry's. Though Sophie didn't care much for Larry's, she frequented the joint because of Puss's affiliation.

When leaving Larry's one evening with Sophie in tow, Puss was confronted by another young fellow.

"Robbie? Robbie, is that you? … No fucking shit, man! Robbie Robertson! How the hell are you?"

Puss tried to ignore the comments and quickened his pace until Sophie took hold of his arm to halt his progress, "Puss, that man knows you. You should answer him."

Puss stopped dead in his tracks to invite conversation.

The other young man approached, "Robbie! I haven't seen you since high school! How've you been? How's your mom? … Don't you recognize me? … It's me, John Shaler… Come on, Robbie, we've known each other since we were four years old!"

Puss replied, "You must have me mistaken for somebody else," and began to walk away.

The other young man, John Shaler, continued to speak, though his words were lost as Puss dragged Sophie away.

When the couple arrived home a wee bit later, Sophie began questioning Puss. How did this man know his name, or his fake name, whichever, if Puss didn't know him? How could this man know Puss from high school, for most of his life at that, if Puss came from Ireland? How?

Puss gave no answers. He shrugged it off and slapped

Sophie across the face when she would not desist.

Three days later, while Sophie was at work and Tad was at school, Puss and his evolved set of belongings disappeared.

Sophie would not accept the obvious explanations. *Too many false prophets, eh?* And it made not a bit of difference to Tad.

The MetGo products, buried behind boxes in storage, soon came out. Par standard, to say the least. The knives were dull, though never used. The oils had gone rancid. And the home-brewing machine simply did not work.

Alas, Sophie realized she'd find no man to help her turn water into beer, let alone wine. So she took the easy route and bought it all pre-made. She turned to the bottle, forgetting she had a past, a future, a son, or a liver.

Feel pity for Tad yet?

Poor boy, lost his daddy, lost his Dob Barley, his Puss, even his mommy; it's all a si(g)n—right?

Don't pity Tad though, 'cause those folks were never his to begin with, but he needed an exemplum. And, by God, he'd found more than one!

What better examples to start anew. Even though life had no chance of comprehendible definition, it had more than enough chances for redefinition. The turn of a corner could redefine a person! The drop of a hat could redefine a person!

Truth, lies, circumstance—anything.

Was that the ticket?

Tad fancied himself starting over. Somewhere else. As someone else. He thought of picking up and leaving town—storming right the hell out of this place. He didn't know for sure where he'd go, but he expected it'd be somewhere really awesome.

He'd always been a fan of cooler temperatures and

climates, though not too fond of snow. Fall was his favorite season. So he figured he'd go somewhere where it was always some type of autumn year-round. And it'd have to be somewhere nearby to some major body of water, preferably sea over fresh. That's where he'd go for a fresh start, a do-over—where he'd redefine, refine, himself in both the most ideal and the most absurd terms.

He wouldn't stutter when he talked to strangers, and he'd actually have the nerve to overcome the embarrassment that has long prevented him from buying a few seasons of "The X Files" on DVD.

Maybe he'd tell people that he was a 23-year-old single fellow who moved to this new place after giving up a rather unpromising interior design career somewhere in mid-state Georgia; that he left it all behind to move here to this new place in pursuit of his perfect "soul mate," with whom he connected online in a chatroom called "Christian Singles 2"; that he left to be with her, only to find out that she was really a 15-year-old boy with a creative streak, a propensity to fib, and a very heartless sense of humor; that now, now, his only aspiration was to do something more meaningful with his time, maybe get a job delivering polar water or working in the HVAC industry. And he'd tell everyone to call him "Olive." *Maybe get a tan and dye my hair red, like a pimento.*

Or maybe he could just be Tad—but a different Tad. Maybe some booze would loosen him up. A little pot, the occasional line or two of cocaine. He could pick up chicks and fuck them, maybe give them a slap or a punch every now and then. Baggie jeans and porno magazines.

The possibilities were endless! And they were there. He just needed to make his selection—for one thing was certain, he couldn't keep being the same old Tad, not after she was gone. He'd have to do something. Anything.

Right?

~ 10 ~

When she first moved in with Margo and David, all those years ago, Margo was quite restrictive about what she could bring with her from her home, "You'll bring no posters, no childhood toys that you've outgrown. Be sensible, dear, bring only your valuable things. Your mother had poor taste—just look at your things! Such cheap furniture! What gaudy trinkets! I'll have none of that in my home."

Her bedroom furniture set, if one could call it that, as it was a collection, an eclection, of different pieces with no binding theme, was left behind, as were nearly all of her knick-knack possessions—those "gaudy trinkets," as Margo would say.

The 12-inch ceramic poodle that she found at a yard sale, her lighted swan snow globe, her family of stuffed animal unicorns, and the jack-in-the-box, with a jack in the likeness of her beloved Phantom from "Phantom of the Opera," never found their way to Margo's house. In fact, most of her things didn't. Not even Mollie.

But these, these, these were the things she cared about most—the things she was proudest to own. They had long provided her comfort and joy. But, like comfort and joy, they had no place in Margo's home.

These things now lived solely in her memories, her dreams.

The only things that Margo allowed her to bring, or that Margo appropriated on her own, were some of the more practical things—some of her clothes, mostly undergarments and outerwear since, according to Margo, most other of her clothing was "quickly going out of style" or "too worn" and needed to soon be replaced; any and all jewelry, genuine or costume but not jejune, since jewelry always had worth, even if only market, in Margo's world; some of her parents' dish- and silver- ware, just so that Margo could have back-up sets to use for the least formal of fare; random vases, platters, decanters, and decorative bowls—those few and far things which Margo deemed to have some esthetic or, at the very least if not at most, probable resale, value.

Then, there were the books. Margo gathered every hard-bound book from every room in the house and invited them to her home. The softcover books, mostly pulp novels and children's literature, were tossed aside. Granted, most of the hardcover books were of the same ilk as the soft—hardcovers purchased before their more pliable counterparts were released. But Margo had a remedy for this.

From each volume of hard pulp, Margo removed its descriptive jacket and replaced it with a sleeve of blank mock leather she bought from a local book-binding store. Book after book, hard-bound lest you forget, garbed in the same shit-stain-brown coat. These properly dressed books found their way to Margo's den, filling the gaps in the severely outdated sets of legal texts that hid behind the glass doors of either of the two antique barrister's bookshelves that flanked both sides of the fake fireplace with electrically illuminated logs.

What items Margo saw as paltry or passé were donated to thrift stores as the necessary precursor to a welcomed, albeit cooked slightly past medium-rare, tax deduction—Margo itemized, of course. All other things were put to an auction, the proceeds of which were used to redecorate Margo's spare bedroom and bath to accommodate a girl in her teen years the way Margo saw fit. Ah, and that was precisely the problem: her bedroom was neither decorated nor intended "for" her but merely "to accommodate" her "presence" in Margo's home.

Even now, this room was not really hers. It was just a room that hid her and her things away from the rest of the world. Her belongings were stored in the drawers of a dresser and a desk that were not hers. Her clothes hung on hangers that were not hers in a closet that was not hers. Any sign of her was neatly tucked away behind and within the implements of Margo's design.

In modern parlance, the word "bedroom" implies something more than a room with a bed or a room where one sleeps. It implies a sense of ownership, a sense of possession. A sense of home. She did not have these feelings in this room. This room was not her bedroom.

True enough, she did sleep there. She did lay her head to rest on pillows fluffed by a forced hand. To her, maybe it was more like a hotel room—perchance an inn, possibly one in some rich northeast state where young couples would flee to forget who they were and all that they had or hadn't done. If only this room could do that for her.

But, unlike those young couples, she had no home to which to return. For her, this room was a place of neither reverie nor retreat; it was a place that imprisoned her in its unfamiliar confines, constantly reminding her of those things she did not, and may never, have.

Even if this room didn't provide for her that same sense of refuge it would provide a young couple on holiday, it still had the outward visage of a quaint little room in some quaint little inn.

With one turn of the brass knob, she, the imposed and permanent guest in Margo's home, would enter a quietly pastel world peppered with large furniture made of oak, maybe pine, doused in floral print fabrics and off-white lace. Some might have called it "Country French," though she never used the term.

It was a room of generically medium size, with a rose-colored area rug centered atop wall-to-wall grey Berber carpeting. To the left of the entry door, there was a short pale wooden dresser, some three feet high, with a broad mirror, framed in that same pale wood, affixed from behind.

On the dresser's top were usually few things. A mirrored beauty tray, reflecting the bottoms of perfume bottles never used—aside this, a gold-plated brush and comb which dare not touch hair. A large crystal bowl—but not one from her parents' house—filled with whatever potpourri was seasonally correct at the time.

The dresser stopped two feet away from the corner where its hind wall met the next wall, the latter feeding into a narrow closet door. In the apex of the corner, there were three corner-cut shelves, each housing a white porcelain bell of similar size and design but with a different flower painted on each bell's stomach.

Inside the closet, her clothes hung on thick wooden hangers. Blouses and shirts were on the left side of the closet, minimizing the length any item could hang in order to make room for a stout wicker hamper purposed to swallow her dirty clothes. Trousers and long skirts hung to the right, with a gap of space between the extent of their hang and the shoe rack below. Jeans and sweaters were folded and placed, along with the occasional hat, on the shelf atop the rod line.

Inched appropriately past the closet door, with its headboard flushed to the wall, the four-post queen-sized bed jetted out to occupy a significant portion of the room. The bed's body was of the same pale wood as the dresser, the same pale wood as the shelves and all of the other furniture, and its attire strived for that layered look—linen on top of linen, pillow on top of pillow.

The duvet? A cream base with lilting floral bursts fair in hue—yellow, light blue, pink, and purple—and interrupted only by two rectangles of finely-woven navy blue cord, one to outline the parameters of the mattress' field and the other to purse the ends of the duvet as it spat out a stream of ruffled cream lace from all sides but its head. Beneath the lace frill, there was a pleated navy bed skirt that remained motionless one inch above the floor.

Cast at the foot of the bed, between the two base posts, was a bench. It was as tall as the mattress' height and had a navy blue fabric top with a needlepoint floral design much bolder than that of the duvet. This bench was always empty until nightfall, when the duvet and the excess of linens and pillows would be carefully folded and there placed for safe harbor until morning.

A small nightstand, with nothing more on its surface than a petite crystal wind-up clock and a gold-plated bedside lamp shaded with a frosted glass half-bulbous head, stood against the next corner of the room, some slight distance to the left of the bed.

The next wall was almost entirely of windows. Six double-paned windows with a modest sill below. Six double-paned windows, each nearly five feet high with only two inches of wall five times disrupting their succession. A pair of clean white vertical blinds, each sheltering three windows in its own right, cascaded down the length of the windows. Next in turn were three ruffled lace panels, cream of course, one flowing into the next so as to appear seamless. The final dose of this window treatment consisted of a set of drapes, always drawn back, with their exaggerated ends rippling upward and inward in narrowing width and shortening height until reaching the two center windows where a flight of downward-pointed parabolic swells bellied out from behind and tapered up to the acme of the carefully covered curtain rods.

The print was a familiar one, seen only a few feet away covering the bed. That same cream base, with those same floral bursts. Fair in hue. The only interruptions by that same finely-woven navy blue cord. That navy blue cord, once, to mark the curtains' most outward vein. That navy blue cord, again, four inches apart from its brother thread, stitching a comber that leaked familiar ruffles of familiar cream lace.

A shorter, fatter version of a wing-backed chair straddled the next corner. It was upholstered in maroon velvet, to compliment, perhaps counteract, the otherwise pastel palette of the room. Placed in front of this chair was what, for all obvious intents and purposes, appeared to be an ottoman. Four wooden legs, curved out at the ends, one small drawer in its boxed body, and a cushion top of velvet like in kind to that of the chair. But, upon further inspection, this was more than a mere ottoman.

The cushion top could be lifted up and left to rest on two hinges at its one end. What was inside was an interesting thing indeed!

A discrete cavern had been painstakingly hollowed out a few inches beneath the linear cut of wood that supported the cushion top. In the center of this secret ambit, there was a metal plate fashioned to the form of a shoeprint, propped up by tiny metal bullets that adhered to their wooden floor. A shoeprint. To either side of the shoeprint were small built-in compartments of various sizes.

Indeed, as it was, this ottoman was none other than a glorified apparatus to shine one's shoes! That shoeprint was where one would rest his or her foot. Those compartments were where one would keep his or her shoe shining equipment and accessories. Perhaps a smooth cloth. Leather polish. A brush with soft bristles. *We must be careful not to scuff.* Oh, this really would come in handy, quite handy, if she knew how, or wanted, to shine shoes.

A few feet away from this chair and its unusual accoutrement was another door, the third door visible from the room's interior. On the other side of this door was a small but conveniently accessible bathroom. Cool white and baby blue tiles checkered the bathroom floor. The blue tiles dropped out of the game as soon as floor creased with wall and their cool white equivalents slyly crept a few feet up around each of the four walls. Above the tile, the rest of the wall was covered with a gold-dusted off-white wallpaper regularly patterned with rich gold silhouettes of horn-blowing plump angels of indeterminate sex.

The main attraction in this tiny bathroom was its white porcelain commode with its proper brown shag toilet seat cover atop its always closed lid. There was usually a bowl of potpourri placed on top of the toilet's tank, although it proved somewhat impractical as the bowl's girth faintly exceeded the depth of the tank such that one who went potty there would have to lean forward a bit in order to avoid feeling the bowl's scalloped edges prick at her back or to avoid, worse yet, knocking the bowl over with some usual advance.

The commode sat beside a standing sink with a proudly arched faucet and oval mirror set above. Across from the sink, on the other shoulder of the door, was an adequately-sized stall shower with a pocked glass door. A brown shag shower mat.

The left end of the shower fed into a built-in cabinet that stretched its way to the back wall. The wood doors of the cabinet were painted off-white, with inset panels sporting the same divine wallpaper found on the walls. These doors successfully concealed the washcloths, towels, and toiletries that resided within. A half-dome frosted ceiling light encircled by a thin gold metal ring illuminated the lavatory.

The door to this bathroom was always kept shut—for there was no need to see into this private realm unless nature necessitated one's presence there.

Back on the Country French side of the door, a final piece

of furniture sprawled the remainder of the last wall—an old-school roller-top desk. The roller-top's top's curl resonated with the curves, bulbs, and swells that characterized this room and conveniently hid those things kept within, although those things kept within were buried even deeper in the many drawers and yawning tray shelves that recessed inches back from the desk's writing pad.

Such was the décor of this room that was not hers. Quite quaint indeed—this room, like a quaint little room in a quaint little inn. How painfully vacant this room was. How it lacked all those things one's "bedroom" usually has. No trace of either personalty or personality. Unmistakably and unyieldingly austere. And so she was required to maintain this room.

Since her earliest days in this house, she was employed, in no literal sense, as the room's chambermaid. She was told that this room must always appear tidy and untouched.

Her bed was to be carefully made each morning, with the navy blue cords of the duvet perfectly aligned and each pillow habitually placed. If she were to sit on her bed during the day, she was to make sure that those lines of navy blue cord did not yield into wrinkles once she removed her weight.

Her clothes belonged only in the closet, the hamper, or the drawers. Clothes were never to be tossed on the floor, laid out on the bed, or stacked on the bench. All other belongings, of whatever and any kind, had to be kept in drawers when not being used.

Oh, how the surfaces of her furniture could hold nothing but those few items that Margo selected—those unused perfume bottles, that unemployed brush and comb, and those bells that never rang. Each of her things had its place, but that place was where no one could see them. Out of sight, out of mind—by more than chance, the way Margo and David thought of her.

But tonight was a different night. Tonight, she hadn't played by the rules. She so blatantly failed to play her role as chambermaid. Instead, tonight, for what was more than likely the first time, this room vaguely resembled an actual bedroom. It was scattered with belongings, vibrant with possession.

Perhaps the drawers vomited?

Indeed, tonight was a different night. It was to be her last.

~ 11 ~

Tad sat in the maroon velvet chair, leaning forward over his sprawled legs with his elbows resting inches above his knees. His posture was as tight and rigid as the panic and anxiety that bolted against his nerves.

He eyed the wonders of her room, frightened by how it had been enlivened. Hidden things had found their ways to the surface; buried pieces had been unearthed.

Naturally, this room was not dirty. It was merely messy, clattered with clusters of her custody. There was, however, something unsettling about this display of personalty. Something gruesome and something absurd.

Her favorite black polyester suit and purple satin blouse were carefully folded and placed atop the bench at the bed's foot. A small, rectangular jewelry case, of crushed blue velvet rimmed in shiny yellow gold, was carefully laid out on top of the ensemble and dented only a fraction of the satin's glean.

Inside the jewelry case were her cherished set of silver pearls with its matching set of silver pearl earrings and matching silver pearl ring set in antiqued 10-karat gold. When she requested this jewelry set as a birthday gift, Margo refused, swearing hued pearls were cheap, until she saw a nationally syndicated female anchor wear something similar on the evening news.

Her trusty black sandals, which she almost always wore, were centered below the bench.

The surface of the un-rolled roller-top desk, a few feet away from and a few inches behind where Tad sat, brimmed with discrete licks of piled books, full little boxes, and filled paper bags.

The dresser had met a similar fate. Some folded things that were probably scarves or handkerchiefs, a set of four shot glasses (one, chipped) in the shape of tiny guitars, a clear- and blue- glass penguin figurine, and a cherry-wood trinket box waded between a sparse colony of additional books, boxes, and bags. *Where had all these things been hidden? This room couldn't have had enough drawers.*

All of these items seemed so carefully placed, so methodically and deliberately arranged. What life they brought to this room was an unnatural one. Those of her possessions that had been laid out had a purpose other than expression, convenience, or flare. They were not meant to bleed grace.

Instead, they'd been programmed with something else in mind.

Each stack of books, each box, and each bag—the folded scarves and kerchiefs, the shot glasses, penguin, and trinket box—were all adorned with tiny pieces of yellow paper. *Post-it® notes.* There were words on each paper. Although Tad sat too far away to read the scrawled characters with any specificity, he knew what they were.

These things are her will, her last will and testament.

Indeed, what Tad knew, without reading, was that each little yellow note bore a name along with a telephone number and/or address. She had so recorded the designees of her tangible wares.

The last of her written decree lay inches away from the bed on the nightstand, held in place by the heavy base of the petite crystal clock—a note, roofing the blood leather-bound spiral notebook in which she regularly scribbled down appointments, contact information, and residual thoughts.

The note, on loose-leaf paper with the tattered ends torn away, read:

in wake of *water*

Margo and David:

Thank you for allowing me to stay with you all of these years. You've given me a bed to sleep in and provided me with food. I've tried all these years to not ask much of you. But now, I have a few things to ask. I hope that you will do these things for me. It would mean a lot.

All about my room, you'll find stuff that I've laid out. There are some things in boxes or in bags and some things just sitting here and there. And there are some books. I've put a note on each and every thing to let you know where it should go after I leave. All the notes have the name of the person to whom I want the item to go and have the telephone number or street address where that person can most easily be reached. Please make sure that these people get these things.

Beneath this note, you'll find my notebook. In it, I've listed the names and telephone numbers of all the people, who you probably don't know, who you should contact to tell that I've gone. I've left some other instructions and information in the notebook as well.

I hope I'm not asking too much. Please do these things for me. It's the way everything should be.

Thanks again for the housing and food. I'm off now to find myself. I doubt we'll meet again. Farewell.

The centerpiece of this room was the most delicate and intricate display. Her. *Her.* In an uncharacteristic pants and top set of faded crimson red, with her long waves of hair pulled to a tight ponytail at the back of her head, she laid at a limp haft-mast on her tautly made bed.

Her hair was subtly darker than usual, damp but very clean. *Freshly bathed.* It glistened with a smooth, tight moisture she couldn't have intended. Her skin looked rosier than its norm, perhaps reflecting, refracting, or absorbing the red fabric that covered most of her body.

She looked like a larger-than-life ragdoll carefully positioned on a showroom bed. The layers of pillows, which Margo religiously required, supported her from the width of her shoulders to the small of her back, propping her torso to a backward lean. Her arms laid, with juxtaposed ease, to each side of her frame—palms up and fingers curled, as if waiting to catch Jesus's, or God's, precipitous reignfall.

Her legs extended outward from the apex of her sex, gradually widening to her duck-pointed bare feet.

In the gape of her legs, near her knees and at a logical toss-point from her left hand, lay an empty fifth of Vladimir™ Vodka. Between her knees, the bottle appeared as the waist of a capital letter "A."

Her, her own scarlet letter. She, her body forming the letter to spell out her own sin. "A" for "absurdity." But not even Hawthorne would weep.

She had finalized her arrangements with Tad earlier that day after she woke. She would leave the front door unlocked, and he was to come to her room, unannounced, at 7:00 p.m. He had arrived promptly to find everything, including her, in this state.

When he entered the room, she was the first thing he noticed—her head tilted back to rest on only the ruffles of the topmost pillow shams. Just the ruffles of the shams, not the pillows themselves—because of how she was placed on the bed, and by the sheer number of pillows under the length of her back, her head could only dangle unsupported.

She heard his entry and lifted her head, "Tad? … Sit down. I need you to [*too?*] … I need you to [*too?*] … I need you to sit here, here with me… Sit here with me," her speech was already at a lulled slur.

"I took some pills and then drank that vladka… vodka. Some pills. The good ones… Good pills with some vodka… It'll work. It'll work best to let me escape this body."

Good pills and vodka, the coconspirators to her escape.

"The pills'll, and the vodka, the pills'll numb the body. Let my soul get out on its own. Not like slits wrist… slit wrists… where the door is already open. Too messy and I'm already clean. Good pills though."

He hadn't immediately noticed the small tan prescription pill bottle that hid to the side of her right hip. The lid was off, and the bottle was empty. He couldn't see the lid anywhere. *Maybe she'd swallowed that too.*

"But, tanks Thad, or should I say, 'thanks Tad'? … Oh, I meant it the other way around. Backwards. I try. Thanks for coming here, that's what I meant… I try to be funny and make people smile. Stay here Tad, till it's undone, done… done?"

He couldn't stand to look at her as she spoke. With each word, she tried to hold her head up so that she could look at Tad, or so that Tad could look at her. But the pills and the vodka had already worked the earliest of their tragically magic spells on her body. The seduction of her neurons. The rape of her sarcomeres. As she'd try to hold her head upright, it'd invariably and involuntarily fall back to linger above the pillows. The harder she tried to hold her head up, the harder it fell back.

Tad hated that her head didn't, couldn't, reach the pillows. He thought of lunging at her, grabbing her by her bare feet, and roaring like a lion as he pulled her body a few inches farther down the bed to drag her into a spot of comfort.

Her neck and head, and it's subparts in turn, were the only parts of her body that moved. The rest of her, possibly already lifeless, was fixed in position.

Her sounds were even more sickening than her paralyzed pose and obtusely animated head. The words she spoke were affronted and slow, lost in each other and far from crisp. The sound of her voice clanged with pellets of rattling emptiness. She sounded like Death talking in the wind.

But what was worse than her slur, and worse than the relaxed nasal "nnn" noises that swam the suspensions of her speech, was the sound of her breath as her head shifted back and forth.

She made a barely audible startled gasp, consisting of a trinity of rapid inhalations in heightening volume and speed, each time her head unwillingly dropped back. When she triggered her head forward again, she'd quickly and loudly exhale as if she'd either found some sense of relief or just ran an exhaustingly big race. This cycle of breaths interrupted her at midsentences and midwords and flecked her bouts of nasal resonance.

Her sounds were the most odious when she spoke with her head tilted back above the pillows. Her back-hanging head allowed her mouth and throat to be almost straight in line with each other instead of at their normal near-perpendicular bend. *Perfect position to deep throat, some might say. Not me.* Nearly perfectly aligned, her throat and mouth were like one damp cavern slowly dehydrating over time. Perfunctory glottal gestures echoed moistly before escaping as dry tones. The air in her throat reverberated into heavy stuttered breaths.

Neck drawn back like this, there must have been some pulled strain on her vocal cords—for certain syllables sung out in a different key, some flat while others sharp. *Dissonance and discord.*

"There's one last thing, Tad… Ting, Thad. I have to-tell [*total?*] you. I have to tell you something… One thing. I'm sorry." She was holding her head up now, her eyes squinting beneath their weeping lids.

Drunk eyes.

"I'm just sorry. Don't ever think… Think. It was never your fault. You didn't make it happen. It just happened… at the wrong time. But… I'm sorry… Sorry that it was me."

What? This isn't my fault. Nothing of this is my fault. "A" for "absurdity"—hers, not mine.

"You know. Really," head back, trinity gasp, quick jerk, climactic puff, "it doesn't suit you. This guilt… It's not your fault. I wish you'd never seen me… that you'd had nothing to tell."

Tad's form coiled with unease and confusion. *What guilt?* He felt a light hollowness in his stomach and a tingling in the soft inner-corners of his elbows and knees. *Wish I'd never seen her?*

"Just stay here, Tad. And, don't say goodbye… You didn't kill anyone. And, you didn't… you didn't kill him."

What? Who?

It hit him like a sonic boom, a tidal wave, and many other bad clichés. Ancient demons were awakened, extinguished memories burst once again into flames, to make sense of her words. He knew of what she spoke.

~ 12 ~

Flash back to one year more than ten years ago, weeks before Tad's father died. She, 15 years old. He, a mere 10. She'd sat for him most of the day since his mother was on 12-hour rounds at the hospital that week.

His father, Reverend Linders, came home a little later than usual that mild summer's night, somewhere on the crest between late evening and early night. She, Tad, and the good Reverend ate ice cream and watched television for a while.

Tad's bedtime drew near. His father stood tall, "Tad, it's time for you to go to bed." Tad, hesitant to leave the good times they three'd been having in the living room, slowly stood up with a shrug, "Okay."

The Reverend nudged Tad's shoulder, "Make sure you brush your teeth."

She remained seated on the couch as Tad ascended the stairs. The Revered leant over and picked up the three ice cream bowls, each filmed in the light syrup that is the unattainable last bite for even the staunchest of sugar fiends. He looked down at her, "Want more?"

"You know I do," she suggestively smiled.

Tad, plump little 10-year-old child that he then was, was very upset and resentful that she'd get more ice cream while he had to go to bed. Why hadn't he offered Tad more?

It was ice cream—and candy, and television, and toys— that defined how fair life was at this time. Justice ran on batteries and electricity, served in bowls and covered with sprinkles. The cruelty of the world was when one got what another craved.

Why couldn't he have more ice cream? Why did he have to go to bed? It didn't seem fair.

Nonetheless, he finished his stride to the top of the steps, brushed his teeth, changed into his sleepwear, and went to bed.

Tad was restless that night. He tossed and turned. It had been a couple hours since he'd gone to his room, and now he was entirely awake. He was mad. He kept thinking of ice cream and chocolate syrup. She got the more he wasn't even offered. He decided to rebel, to act out against the system— he would sneak through the guise of darkness to make sure that justice, and ice cream, was served.

He was too juvenile and convoluted in justifying the late night snack he was about to have. He felt that he was limited, as if he were being deprived of something of which he didn't already have more than enough, and controlled while some- one else, she, got something neither earned nor requested.

For him, this snack would show them, though they would not see it while it happened, that Tad alone would limit and control when he had had enough. He would show them that, when something was not offered, he was man enough to take.

His reasoning was off. Before this night, late night snacking had already become Tad's excessive habit. He was always hungry and had already begun to turn into the chub that he would be for a few more years before dropping a great deal of weight in his mid-teen years. Though he tried to shade his motivation, he really just wanted food. He really just felt hunger, jealousy, and greed.

As was his custom, he slowly crawled out of bed and crept to the top of the landing to listen for any sounds of life on the floor below. His mother was still working, and he wondered whether his father had gone to bed yet. He peeked half of his head out from the half-wall on the landing. There were no noises below. No television. No conversation. No dishes being washed. It was now safe for him to go downstairs for his just dessert.

He tiptoed down the steps and inconspicuously rushed through the living room, sneaking under the arch that bled into the dining room and turning the corner to enter the kitchen. The three dirty bowls and spoons were still sitting in the kitchen sink. In an attempt to conceal his snack from his parents, he took one of the dirty bowls, and one dirty spoon, from the sink to use as the instrumentalities of his mission.

Spoon and bowl in hand, he slunk to the refrigerator-freezer where he dug the used spoon into the same square of vanilla ice cream from which his father had earlier drawn. He shoved quick, awkward scoops of ice cream into the bowl and sucked on the spoon as he placed the container back into the freezer.

He next withdrew the chocolate syrup and drizzled most of what was left in the bottle onto his growing indulgence. Excited that he was getting away with yet another late night rendezvous, he put away the near-empty bottle of chocolate syrup and began devouring his righteous treat with bestial ease.

He downed the snack quickly, right there in front of the refrigerator. He soon finished, but for the wet representative of that unattainable last bite, and placed the once-again used bowl and spoon back in the sink.

The back of his head started to throb. He had a head rush from eating the ice cream too quickly. For him, the best cure for this brain-freeze was always a glass of lukewarm water.

He reached for the drinking glass that always donned the right side of the sink and slowly, carefully turned the faucet ever so slightly to allow a slow, weak stream of water to trickle down into the glass. As he stepped back from the sink and drew the glass to his lips, he heard a thud. A thud, followed by laughter and words.

Two voices.

At the other end of the kitchen, there was an open passageway that led to a mudroom with two doors. One door was the backdoor to the house. The other door led to the Reverend's at-home office.

Tad was perplexed to have heard two voices. Was it later than he'd thought? Was his mother already home? Curious, he had to inspect the scene.

He walked across the kitchen, through the short passageway, and to the door of his father's office.

He leant closer to the door and again heard those two voices. Though one voice was his father's, the other voice was not his mother's. And the voices sounded different now. They were only half speaking.

By age 10, Tad was a master at sneaking around the house and having his fleshy form go unnoticed. He knew how to work the rooms in this house—how to walk over floors or up and down steps without being heard, how to turn handles and open doors without making noise. This too, he had considered an exercise of power and control over himself, if not over his parents and the house itself.

He tugged at the bottom of his pajama shirt and drew it up to the doorknob of his father's office. He held the cloth of it in his right hand as he turned the knob, to muffle the metal sounds that the doorknob usually made. He allowed the door to open an approximate inch and peered through the crack. And then he saw the source of the noise.

The noise was coming from two figures by the Reverend's desk, which was against the right wall of this room, right in the beam of vision created by the door Tad'd opened in his prowling.

She was there with Tad's father, there with the Reverend,

in his office. Completely naked, bent over his desk. The Reverend stood behind her, his black trousers down around his ankles and his basic blue button-down shirt still on and waving over her backside as he slowly moved back and forth.

Her elbows and forearms rested against the Reverend's desk, palms pressed down and occasionally clawing at the desk, her long hair flowing over her shoulders and spilling onto the surface beneath. Each strand of her hair seemed to move to the Reverend's rhythm. Long strands of hair slightly swaying back and forth in a choppy, constant tempo as she tilted her head and glanced back to her left to see the man behind, and inside, her.

His hands were tightly clasped at her hips, his knees slightly bent.

Their voices, which seldom sounded, were hushed to a quietude lower than their heavy breathing. When she spoke, she spoke in letters rather than words, pleasurably-pained a's, m's, f's, and h's. These could have been the beginnings of words she was too flustered to pronounce, or maybe the beginnings of words she was too ashamed to utter in front of the Reverend.

Reverend Linders intermittently spoke full words, usually one word at a time—mostly affirmations, "Yeah," and some form of misplaced prayer, "God." His words were buried deep in panting gnarls that slicked over his curled upper lip.

There was a roughness to what they did, a slow, hard roughness that shone through their unhurried thrusts. Their pulse was slight but strong—clenching, throbbing, like a tightly screwed pendulum tapping against a brick wall intersecting its arc too near to one end; the wall fencing out the majority of the pendulum's predictable swing and making the pendulum thump the most solid thumps harder, harder, and harder against the wall as if wanting only, though never being quite able, to crash right through it.

Tad saw them. He watched them. He knew what they were doing. He raced with conflicting feelings.

He felt disgust—over seeing them together, over hearing his father use God's name in all of this. His disgust was both exemplified and amplified by what he physically felt. All over his body, his skin tightened, thickened, and hardened—scales of loathing crusting his face, arms, and legs.

But where he felt the tightest—where he felt the thickest and hardest—caused him tremendous angst. He himself grew and swelled at this spectacle. His own breath had already begun to quicken.

He was aroused, a thing which he'd only recently begun to understand at his young age. His entire body stood at full attention. What flowed through his veins, but for at one point, was not blood. It was far too thin.

His disgust and angst mixed with anger and rage. Fury that his father wore someone other than his mother, wore this 15-year-old cunt. Wrath that she, who might've been his friend one day, would sleeve his father.

He was unmistakably turned on and unquestionably turned off. And while the disgust and rage spurred him to run away or yell out loud, it was the stimulation that kept him silently in place. He wanted, *wanted*, to see this.

Just then, the unlikely couple shifted gears. The Reverend's pace accelerated and his lunges belled wider. He drew farther back and plunged further forward with each sway. Their short breaths grew shorter. He threw his right hand off of her hip and let it hang at his side for a brief moment before he reached forward and, collecting most of her long hair in his palm, pulled at her mane to bring her body to a more upright bow. He leant forward and ran his lower teeth up the back of her neck. For the first time in this escapade, he spoke a full sentence, "You're my fucking whore."

He let go of her hair and firmly pushed her back into the bent over position she'd been in only seconds ago. He seemed to slam at her now, his movements more primal than before. Then he slugged down once again, fixed hard and slow once more. Then—his head back, his trinity gasp, his quick jerk, his climactic puff. *His.*

Witnessing these last steps of their dance, Tad had continued to harbor the mixed emotions and sensations that preyed upon his young mind and body. That thin non-blood that coursed through his veins must've affected either his circulation or the solidity of his stance.

As his father both stiffened and limped, Tad's hand, which had all this while been clutching the glass of lukewarm water he'd inconspicuously drawn from the kitchen sink, let loose. The glass fell to the floor and broke. It sounded as the loudest noise Tad had ever heard. He'd broken his own cover.

They both turned to see the slightly open door, with a figure of Tad's height looming in the darkness. The Reverend jolted, and she yelled out, "Dear God!"—yet another misplaced prayer—as her eyes pooled with tears.

"Tad?" his father insisted, "Tad!"

Tad unwittingly pushed the door further open to reveal himself standing there, amidst chunks of broken glass and spilt lukewarm water, while his own alter-ego slowly but surely deflated.

She ran and hid behind the desk, to get out of Tad's sight. Tad's father stood there in shock, his him sloppily glossed and dangling, "Go upstairs, Tad, now!" He reached down and pulled up his pants as he leapt the slight diagonal to slam the door in Tad's face.

Tad turned and ran to his room, hearing bits and pieces of tears and screams. He jumped onto his bed and began to cry.

And, for crying, he again felt angst—this burgeoning young man of age 10 knew that crying was for sissies. Angst bred once more with rage. He turned over onto his stomach and dug his face into his pillow. He yelped a muted yelp and beat his fists against the mattress.

Again, what coursed through his veins was not blood. Again, it was far too thin. Again, he felt himself thickest in only one place. He reached to take his frustrations out on himself, his left hand lowering to the part of him that felt the most alive.

He acted furiously against himself—a hand gripping too tightly, pulling too hard, tears of physical pain now mixed with tears against angst, and of rage, as all became bliss in but one all too brief moment of sweet discharge, sopped up in his already stained bed.

Tad soon stopped crying, only whimpering every now and then, as he drifted off into a crumpled, near didactic haze of pure agony and pure joy. His world was spinning—what was this that he actually felt?

Just then, the bedroom door opened. It was Tad's father. The Reverend was fully clothed again, yet messily so. In his right hand, he carried a bowl of ice cream drenched in what was left of the chocolate syrup.

The Reverend sat at the foot of Tad's bed, "Here, son. I brought you some more ice cream."

Tad didn't move; he stayed lying on his belly and simply said, "Okay."

"Listen, Tad. I don't know what to say to you. I know that you saw everything. You have to understand—God, you're too young to understand. You'll understand when you're older… You're a man, son. You're a man, and men do these kinds of things. You might do it someday. I'm sure my father did, though I never saw it like you just did. But, we're men,

Tad. We're men, and men do these kinds of things."

He didn't know how to respond to his father, "Yeah."

"Men help each other out, Tad. They know how to keep each other's secrets. You have to keep this a secret, son. You can't tell anyone, especially your mother. A lot of men do this, but no one talks about it. You can't talk about it."

"I won't."

"Good. You're a good man, son. Don't tell your mother. Don't tell anyone. It's a secret. If it ever got out, it'd be the death of me. You can't tell anyone, my little man."

"Okay, dad. I won't."

For all that it mattered, their conversation was done. These two men, those two little boys—each recently spent in his own right and way—remained silently situated on the bed until the Reverend spoke again, "Here, eat your ice cream."

"Okay."

The Reverend placed the bowl of ice cream on Tad's nightstand and walked out of the room. Tad stared at the bowl for a bit before he closed his eyes and went to sleep. It all melted away that night. He'd had more than his fill.

Tad awoke the next morning and wondered if the events of last night had all been a dream—perhaps some misaligned wet dream that went dreadfully sour—but when he saw the bowl of soupy melted ice cream on his nightstand, he knew it had all been too real. It had happened, all of it. The unspeakable act. The conflicting feelings. The conversation. The ice cream. It was all real.

He couldn't stop thinking about the night before.

He thought about how his quest for control and confection paved the path to what he'd seen. But for his manly mission to take what hadn't been offered, he wouldn't be in this awful position.

He remembered how that part of him which dictated his gender found decadent delight at the sight of them together and, worse yet, how it erupted with glee when his hand worked below his belly. (That is what he thought about, you know—he'd been thinking about them, together.) He wondered, and worried, how angst and rage could thicken him to joy.

His father's words were still fresh in his memory. "Men do these kinds of things." Men "know how to keep each other's secrets." Cheating, lying—but weren't these things wrong?

Realize, Tad was just a boy with only a working definition of what it truly meant to be a man. From the attributes and actions of the men around him, the men on television, and even from his own natural impulses and ideas, he collected the data to form his hypothesis: Men were powerful, strong, and proud—they showed no weakness and always got what they wanted. This was what it meant to be a man.

And for being this way—for being powerful, strong, proud, and willful—a man was given the reward of a unique capacity for a unique pleasure within a unique region of his body.

Over the past year or so, Tad had thought he was becoming a man. He knew not to cry, and he always went after what he wanted—and hadn't this been why nature allowed him to find his body rewarding?

But now, all those premises on which he'd based his definition, along with his father's own words about the things that men do, tortured him until he cringed at the word "man."

If this was what it took to be a man, he did not want to be one.

He was incredibly overcome by a feeling he'd never felt before. He wanted more than anything for it to go away.

Right then, he made up his mind: he would tell his mother. To him, this seemed the only solution. It was the only way to stop what he was feeling. Bring it to the outside, so that it won't fester within.

He waited in his room for a couple of hours until after his father left the house, went downstairs, and told his mother what he'd seen the night before. Now it was her problem, not his.

The Linderses were respectable folks, you see—so they never let Tad fully witness the handfuls of fights they had from this day on. They battled each other only with whispers and stares.

But they both started treating Tad differently. Neither of them really spoke to him all that much after that day. His mother's silence, possibly brought on by sadness for him having seen what he'd seen. His father's silence, likely because Tad had broken their men's alliance. Hell, at the bottom line, both of his parents' silence was probably fueled by their ire that Tad spat out a secret they both thought better left untold.

Within days, of course, they got a new sitter for Tad—Mrs. Ballow, remember. She could use the extra money to buy yarn and knitting needles. And Mrs. Linders felt pretty confident that the Reverend probably wouldn't fuck her.

A few weeks later, the Good Reverend suffered a massive heart attack in the shower and crawled down the steps to call for help on the kitchen phone. It was there that he died, and there that Tad found him.

~ 13 ~

Return to the present, to the tragic scene of the doped-up ragdoll at the crossroads of her life and her death.

Waking from the daze of memories that had just been roused in him, Tad jumped up and spoke, "This guilt? It was never mine. It belonged only to you."

As soon as he spoke these words, he realized it was too late. It was done. While he had drifted off to recollect what he'd long allowed himself to forget, her head had fallen back a final time, *never to be lifted again*. Her mouth was still slightly open but made no sound. Her eyes, closed. *Done.*

He fell back into the oversized chair. He looked to the ceiling, then to the floor. Maybe he was looking for her soul. *Did it escape? Gone to heaven or hell?*

If he was looking for her soul, he didn't see it.

The guilt was hers. What I felt? What I felt was something else.

He stood up again and looked around the room. He'd never before noticed how the colors in this room made it appear bright even when only dimly lit. He felt woozy and almost fell forward before catching himself.

His mind kept flooding with images of her and his father on that long ago night he'd only just now recalled. He kept hearing her sickening voice ring out with some of the last words she'd said tonight.

The then and the now were shifting and melding in his head. His mind's eye inserted some present into some past, and he saw them together—his father grabbing her by her hair and pulling her back; she, the pale galloping arch against his father's darkening form, turning her head to stare at Tad and breathily moan, "It's not your fault. I wish you'd never seen me… that you'd had nothing to tell… you didn't kill him."

Kill him? I never thought that I… Why would she think that I thought I killed him?

Because I told? Because he died a few weeks after I told my mother what the two of them had done? I didn't kill him. I never thought that. Is that the guilt she thinks I felt?

No. I never felt any guilt over his death. Never any responsibility.

I was just a kid who told a secret about something I'd seen. That didn't kill him. I know it caused my parents pain. But it didn't kill him.

My parents probably thought I was too young to understand how they were acting. They must've thought I couldn't see what was going on between them, the hate and regret that clouded their eyes and voices. But I could. I saw it. I heard it. I knew why they couldn't stand to talk to me.

Hate and regret, pain and silence, because of something I told.

I only told. I didn't do. They—she and my father—were the ones who acted. The responsibility was theirs. Theirs was the guilt.

Her guilt for how she acted.

What I felt was shame. Shame for how I reacted—with my thoughts, my hands, and my voice.

Shame that humbled me against the faults of my own gender. Shame that silenced me, leaving me to watch what I say because I once said what I watched.

I lost the memories but kept the shame. And now, they've both met each other again.

The chunks of broken glass. The puddle of lukewarm water. The bottle of vodka. The little yellow notes. When had this all begun? Where was it all ending?

Flowing, flowing—past and present. Resonance. nnn's. a's. m's. f's. h's. Dissonance. Doped-up and dancing. The chocolate syrup. The prescription pills. Where was the lid? Hair, swaying. Hair, damp and darkened. Two deaths—one little, one real.

His inner temperature was rising, making the air all around him feel cool, cooler, and cold. He walked closer to the foot of the bed, slowly rounding its lower right corner, as he stared down at her wilted visage. His left hand grazed her left foot. *Soft, full, still so warm.*

He wondered what a real man would do.

What would the Good Reverend do? What about John Wayne?

He again thought of grabbing her feet and dragging her form—of roaring like a lion. Oh, to have her hear his lion's roar!

Pity, I never had my turn.

He glided to the head of the bed, where he knelt down on the floor and perched both his hands on the edge of the mattress, his fingers momentarily clutching the finely-woven navy cord of the duvet to his palms before his arms fell to his sides. Knelt to neither pray nor be the Romeo to a miscast Juliet but to pollute his mind with new memories to couple with shame.

Hawthorne wouldn't weep. And neither shall I.

He simply stared at her as if time had stopped, studying every inch of the her that had once been. Sipping the air around her, he felt dizzy, woozy again.

Could he bring her redemption? Could he flush her with life's glow? Maybe something still lingered, something only he could feel or make felt.

To be a man at her bed, when it's too late for comfort and

there's nothing left to save or to take?

He could stand to be there no longer. He wanted to leave. Still dizzy, he rose to his feet. He didn't blink as he looked down at her face.

I found shame and humiliation because of her actions.

Her guilt and my shame, just like escape and release. Escape, like her guilt—the result of one's own selfish acts. Release, like my shame—instigated by the acts of another.

So it follows that she's found her escape—and I, my release.

It was all at her hands. Her, both her self and my other.

He reached his right hand into the front right pocket of his jeans and pulled out two quarters—one for each of her eyes.

~ 14 ~

The evening passed. Followed by an entire day and then another. One more day and several hours. It had been almost four days since Tad'd placed those quarters on her eyes and left her at her death expecting he'd hear of it the next morning. But, in those near-full four days, he had heard nothing.

His mother never came to him bearing the bad news. He'd read nothing of this in the newspapers. No phone call from Margo or from David. No packages, with or without yellow notes attached, had been delivered. There was no gossip on street corners; no rush of mourners stopped him on the streets. Nothing. There had been no reaction.

Was this lack of effect, this lack of communication, some form of acknowledgement, compassion, or respect?

Perhaps, simply, no one told him because they assumed he knew. Maybe Margo or David had surmised that she would have told Tad about this before she did it. They might've known that he'd been there—guessing that he was the one who put the quarters on her eyes, maybe catching his scent in the room or finding a stray hair.

Or, possibly, his mother knew but couldn't stand to tell him. Could be that his mother didn't think Tad could handle it, so she didn't tell him. Eh, Tad and his mother didn't really speak all that often anyway. She was always drunk—maybe she'd just forgotten to mention it?

Maybe the newspapers hadn't publicized this, and the gossipers hadn't gossiped, in deference to Margo's, yes Margo's, impeccable reputation. Ah, and those mourners didn't run to Tad because they didn't want to underscore his friendship with her or offend his preference for brief conversation?

Could be. The aftermath of stillness could've been borne by something with a slight semblance to decency—that air of acknowledgment, compassion, or respect. But it probably wasn't. No, something was very wrong.

Yet, even if out of respect, out of acknowledgment, or out of compassion, however unlikely alike, the silence couldn't remain unbroken for this long. At the very least, there would have to have been some general statement of her passing, some communiqué regarding her funeral or wake. But there hadn't been.

Tad was very concerned. *When is her funeral? Shouldn't it be soon? It's already been four days!* He wondered when he'd get to see her again—for the very last time, laid out in her casket, probably wearing the black polyester suit and purple satin blouse she'd set out on the bench.

He'd seen her in that exact outfit before. Three years ago, when they came upon each other after eight years apart— eight long years that allowed his memory to fade, and his words to retreat, to a point where he was almost safe from, and ignorant to, the rest of the world around him.

He'd seen her dressed like that at Larry's, before the floor acquired its one blue tile, sitting at a booth with five other young adults, three other girls and two boys, all dressed in similarly solemn attire.

Tad, 18 years old at the time, was fresh out of high school and bound to no external obligations. He regularly slept in past noon and was just learning how to appreciate an afternoon of doing nothing but reading books and drinking coffee.

On that day, he decided to go read a book at Larry's, though on another day he might have gone to the park, Betsy's Café, the Quick Mart parking lot, or just stayed home.

He recognized her and her entire entourage—they were all some of the "older kids," each around 23 or 24 years old, each from this same town. Even though he recognized them, he didn't acknowledge them—no waves, no precious hellos. After all, it'd been eight years since she stopped sitting for him, and she probably wouldn't even recognize him now. And those other kids, well, he never really interacted with them before—no need to start now.

He sat down at a booth a few booths away. He pulled out a book, *Pynchon*, and began to read as the waitress, out of habit, came over and poured him a cup of coffee.

About ten minutes went by when he realized that someone had been standing at his table for a while. He looked up from his book and saw her.

"Hi, Tad. Mind if I sit here with you for a bit?"

Instead of replying, Tad glanced up at her, down at his book, to the booth seat across from him, back up at her, and then smiled. She took this as a green light and swooped into the seat.

Tad opened his mouth to speak but then shook his head until his eyes once more found the book he was reading.

She spoke again, notwithstanding his face in his book, "Tracy Lynn's gone and died, Tad. She's dead. Cancer. You remember her, right? We used to be pretty good friends back in high school."

Tad looked up and, slamming his book shut and speaking too slowly, said, "Yeah, Tracy Lynn. I remember her." Tad did, in fact, remember Tracy Lynn, and he'd known that she passed away. He'd read it in the papers and heard a few other people talking about it over the past couple days.

"She was only 24! Just made it past her 24th birthday. That's only one year older than me, Tad! It really makes you think."

"Yeah."

She was chain-smoking long brown cigarettes, *menthols*,

and fidgeting around in her seat.

"I've really got to quit smoking, Tad… Anyway, you're looking good though. You've really grown up a lot since the last time I—since you were younger. I mean, yeah, I've seen you around town all these years. I've watched you grow up from a distance. Ha! That's kinda poetic, 'Tad, I've watched you grow up from a distance!' But, seriously, I have. I'd see you walking down the street one day, and then a couple months would pass, and I'd see you somewhere again. And, I'd think to myself, 'Wow! Look how much taller he's gotten!' or 'I'm glad his acne finally went away.' I'd keep seeing you every now and then, but we were always going in different directions. You'd be going when I was coming or walking on the street when I was in the car. But, now we're right here at the same time, and I thought that maybe it wouldn't be so bad if I tried to talk to you. It's okay, isn't it?"

Eight years. Eight years of recessing into his own world had allowed him to forget any reason he should object to her interaction, "Yeah."

"Oh, Tad, that's great! I can't tell you how happy this makes me."

She must have been waiting for him to reply, with words or some other display of emotion, as she, smiling at him in anticipation, snuffed out her hurried rant to dwell in a fleeting moment of appreciation wherein she didn't exude the verbal chaos which usually characterized her.

Since she was not speaking and because Tad chose to say nothing to her, as normally he chose to say nothing to no one, he flipped his book open again and picked up reading where he'd left off.

Only slightly more than a minute passed before she returned to herself and started speaking again.

"I was at Baker's Funeral Home today. That's where Tracy Lynn's laid out. I ran into the old gang there, and we decided to come down here for a quick bite and to talk about old times. I tell you, Tad, it really shocked me to hear about Tracy Lynn. I mean, I knew she had cancer and all—but, the last time I talked to her, everything seemed okay. I just talked to her not too long ago. Well, maybe it's been a while, about six months.

"I don't remember how I found out that she had cancer. Somebody told me, but I don't remember who. So, I called her up on the phone and just started talking to her. I guess I just wanted to hear her voice—like, maybe I'd hear her voice and know everything'd be okay. So, we're just talking. You know, about 'have you heard from so-and-so?' or 'did you know that this person got a really good job and this other person went to Mexico with her new boyfriend?' Nothing hateful, just normal girl talk. And, the whole time, I'm real nervous because I don't want to say the 'c word.' I'm afraid to ask her how she's been because I don't want to make her uncomfortable or talk about something she doesn't want to talk about.

"Then, she just starts laughing and she says, 'Come on! I know why you called me! Don't be afraid to ask me about what you've heard. I'm not afraid to tell you that it's true.' Now, I'm caught real off guard by that, right, so I say something like, 'I don't know what you're talking about! Heard what?' And, she just keeps laughing and goes, 'Don't you lie to me! I can hear it in your voice.' Then, I say, 'Yeah, Tracy Lynn, you're right. I heard that you have cancer, and that's why I called.'

"She sighs this happy sigh of success, because she was able to pull the truth out of me, and then she says, 'Well, thanks for being honest and thanks for calling. I'll tell you what's up.' And, she goes on to tell me how they found the cancer and how they're treating it and everything else that's going on. And, I'm just amazed at everything she's telling me, and even more amazed at the way she's telling it.

"She's talking in this perfectly calm voice and she's laying it all out the way it is. I'm thinking about how she has this cancer and how she's not whining and crying about it to me. Sure, Tracy Lynn was never one to whine and cry—but, she never had cancer before! And, if someone's going to whine and cry about something, having cancer's sure as hell something to complain about.

"Now, I know that this conversation she and I are having is only a small fraction of the too many days and too many weeks she's had to put up with this, and I'm sure there were plenty of times when she whined and cried about it—because, after all, this is cancer, and she is a human—but, she wasn't doing it now. She was just talking real calm, just being Tracy Lynn. And, to be yourself when something so serious is attacking your body, whether you're being yourself for one or every minute, well, that's saying something."

She waved her hand at the waitress, to signal, in diner patron sign language, that she wanted a cup of coffee. At some point during her monologue, Tad had closed his book again and had zoned in to watch, and listen to, her as she spoke.

"I guess it was strength or hope—probably both—and acceptance that I heard in her voice. It was like she knew that she had this thing, this cancer, that was trying to kill her body, but she wasn't going to die unless and until it actually killed her. It was that whole 'losing the battle but winning the war' kind of thing—like, I could imagine her in some forest carrying a shield and a sword and fighting some big dragon that followed her around everywhere she went. Every day. And, the dragon's all bigger than her, and it has powers and weapons that we mere mortals cannot comprehend—but, there's little Tracy Lynn, jumping around as she keeps facing the dragon. She won't back down.

"I think that's what they mean when they say that, right?

'Losing the battle but winning the war?' The fact that she's dead now just means that she lost the final battle. There were plenty of other battles before that, though. I'm sure. She won the war even though she lost the last battle. She won because she kept being herself and because she's what those close to her will remember, not the cancer. She might not be the type of warrior that will go down in the history books or find herself the subject of a chapter in some treatise on war, but her family and friends will always remember that she was a hero.

"You know what, Tad? I think that, if I ever wrote a book, I'd make sure I mentioned Tracy Lynn. Of course, I'd write about Momma, Joyce, and Papa too. That way, it's like snippets of them can go on living even after their deaths and the deaths of everyone else who knew them. It's the closest thing to immortality that there is, isn't it? A little like cheating death… Okay, I'm getting off track. Let me get back to what I was saying."

Tad couldn't remember the last time anyone had spoken this many words to him at one time. He'd turned his voice mostly inward too many years ago, and the majority of people easily dismissed him or grew short at his propensity for plain pith.

At first, the way that others shied away from his purposefully shy self was quite unfortunate since Tad loved stories. He learnt, however, at a moderately young age, before most kids are avid readers, that books could satiate his hunger for information and entertainment.

He'd read too many books to count by this time, absorbing both fact and fiction. He could read very quickly—quickly enough to finish a 300-page novel in just over three hours.

And now, this pale creature sat before him and gave him word after word. A story. Information. Entertainment.

He was even further intrigued by her speech because

she verbalized something he'd never known how to read on paper. He suddenly realized that every book he'd ever read he had read entirely and utterly wrong.

Her words, her voice, had something far easier to hear than to see. Inflection. Infliction. Affect. Depth. And emotion. She would say certain words louder than others or take some form of character or cinema when she talked in clichés or made analogies. Some words and, or, phrases stood out between pauses and by repetitions.

He wondered—if he were to read, rather than to hear, her words, how would the text appear?

Some sentences, incomplete—mere phrases, at best. And ideas that began with conjunctives and disjunctives. Contractions attached to too many words, to some that should not've been contracted. Perfect participles, the passive voice would have had to've been used from time to time, formed by auxiliaries and cascading pluperfect tenses.

He could hear her commas, her hyphens, ellipses, and exclamation points. Her emphatic devices. He appreciated every word she chose to use, the way she chose to combine them, and the pace at which she spoke.

He'd never seen this emotion, this richness and impact, in any book he'd ever read. Sure, of course, it had been there in those hundreds of books—only, he never saw it. He couldn't comprehend it.

Those books, he'd read for their stories, for their information. He could remember what happened to characters, plot lines, and big conclusions. He had memorized dates, events, and certain ideas. But he could recall nothing of how his league of authors had used, or misused, the English language.

He'd been reading books for only part of their worth. And those stories he remembered, he remembered, and only ever knew, too narrowly. He'd cheated his favorite authors and cheated himself. He would read differently from this day on.

He would read every book as a monologue, as if delivered by some player, as a one-man show, seated on the sole wooden chair on an otherwise empty stage.

He would read every book as a monologue, as if delivered by one person seated across from him in a vinyl booth in a small town diner. *Her*.

He would read every book as a monologue—so that his mind could hear what his quick eyes would gloss over. Words and punctuation would mean more to him this way. He'd remember how his authors wrote, not just what they wrote. He'd find inflection and emotion within, and between, the lines.

"Now, Tracy Lynn and I had been talking on the phone for over an hour, and she tells me that she has some other people she has to call back. So, I just say, 'Okay, Tracy Lynn. I'm glad we got to talk and all. I know you'll be real busy, so you call me back when you get a chance. Or, when you want to talk.' After I hang up, I don't feel so bad anymore. I feel proud of Tracy Lynn, and I hope and pray for the best.

"Maybe three or four months go by, then she calls me and tells me the cancer went into remission. I was real happy to hear that! And, we just go on talking—about other stuff. She's telling me how she's engaged to be married and planning her wedding. Just normal conversation. Really nice. And, we just keep talking until we have nothing left to say.

"All of a sudden it's six months later. I hadn't talked to Tracy Lynn. Figured she was busy planning her wedding. Then, Jim calls me the other night and tells me, 'Tracy Lynn died!' And, I go, 'No way! Fuck you! Her cancer's in remission. You lie!' and I just hang up the phone. But, he calls back and tells me the whole story.

"And, I was so shocked, Tad. Last thing I'd heard was that it'd been in remission. I never knew it came back. But, it did. And, it spread. Poor Tracy Lynn lost a lot of hair and had to get a glass eye. The dragon found her again… So, I'm really upset, and I'm mad that Tracy Lynn died. I go to Margo's den and get the newspaper so I can read the death notice and know when Tracy Lynn will be laid out.

"And, I read the death notice, and it's this really incredible notice. It's telling people to come to the funeral home to 'celebrate her life,' and it's asking them to wear their favorite colors. So, I go down to Baker's today, and the place is packed. And, there's Tracy Lynn in the casket. She's wearing normal clothes, nothing too fancy, and there're all these stuffed animals and pictures in there with her.

"I go talk to Tracy Lynn's mom, and she smiles at me and tells me some of the things that Tracy Lynn went through over the past several months. Only, she's not just talking about the cancer. She's talking about good things too. And, she's talking about the past, about when Tracy Lynn and I were in school together.

"We're talking for a little bit, and I tell her how nice the death notice was. She told me Tracy Lynn's dad had written it. So, then, I'm thinking—since I know that her dad wrote that notice, and I'm talking about both happy and sad things with her mom—the dragon must've chased her parents too. They too won the war but lost the battle. Granted, they lost their daughter—and, that's got to be one of the worst things, if not the worst thing, to lose—but, they have all these colors, this celebration, and 24 years of memories about Tracy Lynn. No way that it's an even exchange. But, they have something else too—they have the pride of knowing that Tracy Lynn was Tracy Lynn and that she was a hero. And, they have the comfort of knowing that she, who suffered too much, finally found an end to her pain.

"It's nothing that can make it entirely right or okay again, but it's enough to make it less wrong. I mean, I still feel awfully bad for them. I know what it's like to lose someone in your family. I know it too well. But, to lose a daughter? I'm glad Momma never lived to see Joyce go. And, I was too young to understand what Papa was going through when Joyce died, and too busy going through my own problems."

Their outwardly one-way conversation started to slow down and taper off, not because Tad had sat there without saying a word for so long but because her five friends from the other table were getting ready to leave.

"Well, Tad, looks like everyone's leaving. I should probably go too. We might head down to Baker's for a little bit more. I don't know. It was nice to talk to you. Really, it was. I'm glad that we can… I'll tell you what. Here's my idea. Let's you and me just start all over again. Okay? Let this be the first day we ever met. No need for introductions, of course. But, let's just start again. Maybe we can be friends? I'm going to the funeral tomorrow morning. Maybe you'll stop by the house, and we can go together?"

That same ignorance that the past eight years had bred, "Okay."

"Great. I'll see you then."

She stood up and walked out with her crew.

Tad remained in his booth and opened his book to the place where he'd left off. But then, he shut it again and reopened it to the first page. *I'll just start all over again and see what this really is.*

Tad did go to her house that next morning and joined her at Tracy Lynn's funeral. After that day, he'd go to her house more and more often and see her almost every day. To a new friendship, they'd both been enticed. He, by her language and how she taught him to listen to what he read. Her, by the forgiveness he hadn't known he'd given her.

Was this the cycle of life? A phoenix rising from another's ashes? Was it Tracy Lynn's death that brought their relationship to life?

No. Tracy Lynn's death had just catalyzed it. What brought it on was another inexorable thing—Time. Time to forget, time to regret, and time to learn. Time to live, to want to live, and to die. Time had separated them and then brought them together again.

How some loathe, some fear, these inexorable things— time and death. How some try to avoid and deny them, but how all fall prey to their designs while few ever really appreciate their worth. From time, and from death, there are lessons to be learnt—yet, the lessons of one are often extinguished by the hands of the other.

What lesson she'd learnt from Tracy Lynn's death must have been lost in time, in the three years that had passed from then to now. *She too knew how to forget.*

Maybe it was this that was life's cycle. A friendship which started on words praising life and ended on words welcoming death.

~ 15 ~

Tad's thoughts shifted from one funeral to another. He again began to wonder about his current predicament. *When is her funeral? Why haven't I heard anything?*

He decided to walk down to Margo's and David's house to confront them. Yes, he would be proactive. If he showed up at their door, they'd have to say something, anything, to him. They'd have to tell him what was going on. What else could they do? Surely even the most skewed splinters of respect, compassion, or acknowledgment would bend if he knocked down their door!

It was the early afternoon of an early autumn's weekend day. *Soft, full, and still so warm.* The sun was somewhere above, casting its light down over this part of the world. The leaves on the trees hadn't yet begun to fall, though they'd started already to change colors and dry at their ends. He blamed gusts of wind for dislodging the few leaves he saw here and there—for he knew the moist veins and stems could not have wanted to abandon that which anchored them down.

The town hummed with its usual activity. Cars drove the streets. People turned corners. Doors opened and shut. The world kept on breathing as if nothing had ever, ever been lost. Not now, not before.

He knew the path he traveled well. He practically bounced through his course, long legs alternately pump-ing the immoveable ground beneath. All those around—the townies, the strangers, the leaves, and the sun—were blind to the veracity and dedication that parented his gait. He was just another person walking on another street, going to some-where where none cared to know. Uninterrupted, uninspiring, but unquestionably there.

He didn't have to think of which way to turn or how far to walk. His body already knew these things. His mind was free to roam—but it couldn't. It fixed on one thought. *I need to find out. I need to find out. Why haven't I heard? I need to find out.*

Any other thoughts that tried to enter his mind flung back to whence they came. He was determined to think, to know, only one thing.

Soon enough, he was in front of Margo's and David's house. He stopped walking and stood on the sidewalk for what felt like an hour, though it had been merely seconds, and stared at their house. He could see a few light bulbs glowing behind the downstairs curtains. He saw a figure, probably Margo's, seated in the living room. Things looked normal, ordinary.

He walked the cement path intersecting the lawn to the two front steps of the house. He took a deep breath and raised his right arm, with his hand tightly fisted, to knock on the door. He knocked five times, in quick rhythmic succession, then twice more. He kept his fist close to the door in case he needed to knock again.

Within moments, Margo appeared at the door. Tad's fist was still raised as if, and in case, he needed to beat the details out of her.

"Good afternoon, Tad."

He lowered his arm to his side then bent it up and reached to scratch his neck, "Hi, Margo."

"She isn't here, Tad. She has gone away. She left the other day."

She's gone. I know that she's gone. But you obviously don't know that I know. Why didn't you tell me? Why didn't anyone tell me?

"It was all rather sudden. She made her decision and went on her way."

I need to know more. When is her funeral? Tell me.

He was dazed by how candidly Margo spoke, as if her not telling him this sooner was no transgression on her part. He wanted information she wasn't giving, so he started to speak: "When…"

"She left the other day. I was just as shocked as you seem to be. It was quite out-of-the-blue. I never knew she wanted to leave so badly."

He started paying more attention to the words she was using.

"It's been awfully quiet around here since she left. We're not used to it yet. David keeps cooking enough food for three."

Tad didn't care to know for how many David cooked. He didn't care to know that the house was quiet or that Margo was shocked.

"I must admit, however, that I am a little bit upset. She's lived here with us for over ten years, and she didn't even inform us of her plans. She simply made up her mind and left without telling us face-to-face. She only left us a note."

Tad's body shivered at Margo's words. *Something isn't right.* He wondered how Margo could be upset by the fact that she didn't "inform them" and not by the fact that she was dead.

Margo chuckled and smiled with linear grace, "Oh, Tad, my apologies! Listen to me! Forgive me. I'm going on and on about how she left, but I'm leaving out some of the most important details. How perfectly morbid I must sound! I'm sorry if I scared you at all."

Yes, important details, morbid. Tell me more.

"She's gone to Venice. She summered there several years ago, after she graduated high school. She made a lot of friends there with whom she's kept in touch, and she's gone to live with them now."

Margo's words seemed to slap Tad in the face. *She's gone to live? No. No. She hasn't. She's died. She's dead. I saw her, dead. Lying on that bed, dead. I put those quarters on her eyes.* Tad felt as though he'd fall over, but he still managed to get a few words out, "But, didn't she…"

Margo cut him off before he could finish his question. Of course Margo cut him off—after all, most people did. Most people didn't want to wait for his slow speech or deal with his compact utterances.

"Whatever you're going to ask, Tad, the answer is almost definitely 'no.' No, she didn't tell us she was leaving. As I've said, she only left a note. I went to her room the other morning. She wasn't there. She left us a note."

No. She was there. She died there. I saw her die there. Something is not right.

"No, she didn't tell us where exactly she would be staying. But, again, like I've said, she had many friends there. I'm quite sure she'll find a safe place."

Tad should have said something. He should've spoken up and shouted the rebuttals and questions that raced through his head. But he was too taken aback, too scared and too confused, to do anything more than stand there in the speechlessness which he knew best. Perhaps for this too he'd one day feel shame.

In any event, he was no match for Margo—even if he did try to speak, she'd cut him off or dismiss him. She didn't answer to him. She answered to no one. *What about God?*

"No, she didn't say when she would be back. In fact, I

don't think she will ever come back. She wrote something in her note about how we wouldn't meet again. I wouldn't hold your breath."

Of course she's never coming back. She's dead. The vodka, those pills. Her body, so limp and so sad. Why won't you tell me? Why haven't you told anyone the truth? What have you done? Something isn't right. You've done something very, very wrong.

You lie to me and tell me she lives. Why?

Tell me the truth. Tell me she's dead. Don't say "Venice." There is no "Venice" for her. Just death.

Tad's body ached because he couldn't say the things he wanted to say to Margo. He simply wasn't strong enough to speak to her, physically or emotionally. He'd lost the will to try.

That ache he felt was cowardliness and fear. No longer a fear that Margo'd merely truncate his verbal attempts, but now a fear of what might happen to him should his attempts actually reach fruition. If he challenged Margo, if he insisted that she had died and told Margo everything he'd seen, what would be the outcome?

Surely, Margo would call him a "liar" or tell him he was "crazy." Margo would never admit that he was right.

What he wanted from Margo were words she'd never say. He saw no point in pressing her for them.

And then there was the chance that hearing Margo deny his truth might make him question his own sense of self. Too great a threat.

Ah, but what of the blaring injustice and disgrace done here? The fact that death had been disguised as distance?

Tad thought of turning and running away. He could go to the nearest authority, the newspapers, or Sherlock

Holmes and tell them what Margo'd said in light of what he himself'd seen. But this too was futile.

No one would believe him over Margo. Margo, the great attorney, could certainly plead a case better than simple ole' Tad.

And, what's more, if he told, there'd be a disagreeable result. After all, once before he had spoken of something he'd seen, and there'd been an unsavory result. Once, he'd unveiled a secret that caused everyone, including him, pain. Could he do that again?

Perhaps the rest of the world, if they believed his story, would somehow hold him accountable—responsible for what he'd seen, even though he, like before, told but never acted. Maybe they'd try to shove guilt, as she had once tried, into the space he allotted for shame. Guilt, perchance, solely because he had not acted. And this he could not bear—to set out on a crusade to deliver the truth, only to end up being cast as the depository for blame.

Speaking up, telling, was no longer an option at this point.

"You look very upset, Tad. I'm sure you are. But, these things happen. You've got to learn to move on… If you'll excuse me now, I have to get going. David and I are meeting some friends in a bit, and I have some things I must do before we leave. Take care of yourself."

Margo looked him once over and then shut the door. Tad bowed his head down and turned away. He wouldn't dare glance back at Margo's and David's house as he started to make his way home.

He walked back the same path that he used to walk there. The sun had dimmed just a little, but the town hummed its same hum. Cars drove the same streets. People turned the same corners. The same doors opened and shut. Yes, the world was the same. It kept breathing as if nothing had gone wrong.

He walked at a lag, his shoes scraping against the concrete and his shoulders hunched, the entire way home. *The concrete was dry—her legacy, gone.*

~ 16 ~

"Damn nigger's gotta pay for what he done, gotta pay for what his parents done too."

Margo sat there, listening as the town sheriff spoke. He was a morbidly obese man. Balding, with topiaries of matted hair sparsely strewn across his oversized head. He had a crooked grin filled with crooked teeth. The words he spoke seemed to spit out of the gaps between his yellowed dentition—proper English, perhaps, lost, decaying, somewhere in the cracks and craters of his teeth.

He smelled of body odor, coffee, and cigarettes. Margo didn't enjoy being there with him, seeing him, listening to him speak. But she had to be there. She had to buy silence.

And the price had been set.

About a year and a half ago, a young girl named Joanie Mills got knocked up—at the ripe age of 14. Joanie Mills, the only child of Professor and Mrs. Mills, two well-known and respected pillars of this fine community.

Joanie was a petite little simpleton who had an amazing duality when it came to sexual matters.

Her entry into womanhood had been a swift one. After she began menstruating around her 13th birthday, she'd felt a rush of sexual feelings and soon discovered how to appease them. Before she was entirely skilled at handling her own self, she took on the task of handling others.

In her mind, it made sense for her to lose her virginity around the time that she started menstruating. Indeed, she thought the two went hand-in-hand, perhaps as if menstruation was God's way of telling her that she was finally ready, and that it was acceptable and natural for her, to now have sex.

She was just a kid—so it isn't surprising that she went crazy like a kid in a candy shop. She took on partner after partner. By her 14th birthday, she'd had intercourse with five different fellows. And with a handful, so to speak, of other boys, she'd had other types of sexual encounters. Mostly boys around her age—but there were a few in their late-teens and early-twenties.

Neither Professor Mills nor Mrs. Mills ever approached Joanie to discuss the reality or morality of sex. After all, the subject was a tricky one, and Joanie was still quite young—they feared that, should they raise the topic, it might actually motivate Joanie to go out and try it. And Joanie never initiated such a conversation with her parents—why waste time discussing theory when one has the chance to practice?

No teacher, no movie projector in a humid classroom, had ever broached the topic since "Sex Ed" was banned from Joanie's school via a petition signed by 90% of the students' parents, including the Millses.

What Joanie learnt about sex, she learnt through experience. Most of her lessons were self-learned or taught by unqualified instructors. Even though she'd developed some impressive skills to satisfy herself and her partners, some basic concepts were overlooked. She knew nothing about love and relationships, and the idea of procreation was over her head—or, maybe, in her palms or throat.

True, she knew that babies could result from coitus—but she didn't know exactly how or why. Her confusion was met only with old wives' tales and young children's myths.

The words of her third "lover," a 15-year-old boy she met at the summer carnival: "Just don't let my stuff get inside you… down there. That's how girls get preggers. I'll pull out before I'm done, don't worry."

Hours after Thanksgiving dinner, her second cousin, her fourth lover, of the same age as she, said, after expelling himself inside her: "Just take a bath. Fill the tub up with hot water, and pour a lot of salt in. Then sit in it for twenty minutes. That'll kill the sperms inside you."

As Joanie work-shopped her sexual skills and awry understandings with these eager and appreciative fine young gentlemen, she felt reassured and accomplished. She felt whole and worthwhile.

Maybe she was trying to recover for some type of loss—taking men inside her to compensate for the fact that her body lost blood monthly. Input for output—providing a sense of balance in her life?

Eh, probably not, since she kept inviting others in far after her monthly cycle was disrupted.

Joanie was nearly five months pregnant before she put two and two together and realized that she was with child. During those five months she had been even more sexually active. At first, when her period didn't come, she thought something was wrong with her womanliness, that something was wrong with her hormones.

And since the word "horny" had to come from the word "hormones," she came up with the malformed idea that maybe, just maybe, her period had stopped because she wasn't "horny" enough. In an attempt to have her period return, she started having sex more and more often—in hopes that her "horniness" would invoke the "hormones" to make her menstruate.

But after five months of being more horny and more active, her period never came! She started to feel sick every morning. Her back started aching. She knew something wasn't right.

Joanie stole a pregnancy test from the drugstore. When the result showed positive, she hid the stick under her mattress and cried before going to the bathroom and filling the tub up with extremely hot water and two full boxes of salt and marinating in it for over an hour.

A week later, she stole another pregnancy test from the same drugstore. She squatted over the same garbage can in the same corner of her bedroom and pissed on this second stick. Awaiting the result, she hoped that her bath had killed the baby inside her.

No such luck, Joanie. The result, again, was positive. She hid the second stick under her mattress—an addition to her growing collection.

Joanie was scared. She didn't know what to do. But she knew she couldn't talk to her parents about this. She decided she'd just wait and see what happened. She decided to eat less food so that the baby would starve inside her. She decided to stop having sex, since maybe a guy's stuff made the baby stronger.

She was fairly determined that the baby would just go away. And if the baby happened to survive, and she had to give birth to it, she'd handle that when it happened. She could drop it off somewhere or throw it away—maybe kill it and hide it under her mattress.

But only a fool believes that she can bury the sins that occurred on her mattress beneath it. Fate, in the form of Mrs. Mills, soon intervened.

Two weeks after Joanie hid the second pregnancy stick under her mattress, Mrs. Mills found it and its predecessor during her monthly cleaning. Joanie didn't know anything about house-cleaning—so how was she to know that her mother flipped mattresses every so often?

By the time Mrs. Mills found the sticks, their results were already faded. Yet, their mere presence gave her reason to confront Joanie.

When Joanie came home from school one afternoon, she

found her parents seated at the kitchen table with cups of coffee and the pregnancy sticks placed in the center of the table like the main course of an uncomfortable family dinner.

"Joanie, are you pregnant?" her father asked.

"Have you had sex?" her mother inquired.

Staring at the faded, smelly sticks, Joanie replied, "Umm, I have… I think I'm… Maybe… I don't know."

Professor Mills jumped up and threw his coffee mug against the wall. Slow brown caffeinated disgust seeped down the canary-colored kitchen wall. Mrs. Mills buried her head in her hands and wept furiously.

Mrs. Mills raised her head, "How far? How far are you?"

Joanie looked perplexed, "Far?"

"How far along are you? When was your last period?" her father clarified as he grabbed her by her shoulders and violently shook her in place.

"Um… I don't know… Five or six… Five or six months."

Her father quickly turned away and slapped his hand against his forehead and shouted, "Five or six MONTHS? Five or six MONTHS? What the hell is wrong with you? It's been five or six MONTHS since your last period, and you didn't think anything was wrong? Joanie, what the hell is wrong with you? You can't be that stupid!"

"I'm sorry… I…"

Mrs. Mills turned her attention to her husband, "What are we going to do? Sweet Jesus, what are we going to do?"

In this town, teenage pregnancy was the kind of thing that could destroy a family's reputation. The Millses would be seen as unfit parents, and Joanie seen as nothing more than a whore. The Millses could not have this! Something needed to be done. So they came up with a plan.

Joanie's parents didn't want to know which young scholar or athlete had wooed their precious daughter into sin. It was better that way, better that they didn't know. For, if their plan was to come to fruition, they couldn't know the beau's name since secrets have a way of coming out and hostilities have a way of materializing.

Of course, abortion was not an option. Joanie was already too far along. Not that it would have been an option in any event since, please note, the Millses are good folks, governed by good old-fashioned ideals, and "abortion" just isn't in their vocabulary.

Their plan was a simple one, really. Mrs. Mills and Joanie would leave town and go to one of those liberal west coast states so that Joanie could bare her child in discretion, away from the town's eye. Once the child was born, they would return home, and the Millses—Joanie's parents—would raise Joanie's child as their own, as Joanie's younger brother or sister.

Joanie's and Mrs. Mills' absence could easily be explained. While they were away, Professor Mills would tell everyone that the Mills ladies went out of town to care for and visit an elderly, dying relative in his final stages of life. And when Mrs. Mills returned with a new baby that none knew she was going to have, the Millses would shrug it off to superstition and compassion.

They'd claim that they didn't inform anyone of their impending bundle of joy because they feared that Mrs. Mills, already in her early-forties, might miscarry or lose the child in the complications of mid-life birth—and to alert others of a potentially risky term and birth would only magnify the loss and grief the Millses and their friends would feel should their baby not make it into this world.

In this light, Joanie's absence made perfect sense—she had gone to accompany her mother and tend to her needs.

Ah, but their simple plan turned out to be anything but simple! When Joanie bore her child, Mrs. Mills cringed. There was no way the Millses could claim this child as their own. This child, a healthy, plump little boy, was not like Professor and Mrs. Mills—this plump little babe was "colored."

"Filthy nigger creepin' up in here, seepin' into our streets and houses. Into our girls too. You let one in and before you know it, bam, they're all up in here. First the coons. Then the spicks. Then God knows what. They gonna come up in here and take our town over, spittin' out half-breed mutts all over the place. No, I aint gonna let that happen in my town. Not while I'm livin'. I'll be the one to stop it. So, you know what you gotta do—make that nigger pay. Make that nigger pay, and I'll take care of the rest for ya'."

The sheriff's coffee had to have been Irish—though his heritage wasn't—because his speech was slightly slurred, and he winced after each sip, "Even if it don't work out perfect, and he don't go to jail for a long while, the shame'll do enough to them niggers. Push 'em outta town, get 'em some dirty looks. We'll get more of a reason to hate 'em, right? We'll say, 'that nigger done raped Joanie, made a bastard child outta that there mutt.' It'll all work out for the better, yours and ours."

Oh, this, the perfect town for those with psoriasis, crabs, or fat bellies—any scratch can be itched. Nothing is too dirty or too out of reach. Every and any thing can be bargained for. Quid pro quo, under-the-table barter, adhesion contracts. Mmm, such pepper for the power-hungry palate!

Joanie refused to put her half-negro child up for adoption. When she saw her baby for the first time, moments after it slid out of her widened vagina, she felt the ridiculous maternal instinct that only a child could feel. She saw the baby as an external extension of herself, a symbol of her maturity and gender. God had given her this baby so that she could be the woman she was meant to be. She felt blessed.

Mrs. Mills plead with Joanie. She begged her child to give up her child. But Joanie would not budge. She wanted only to raise her son. Mrs. Mills could not tolerate Joanie's position and threatened to put the biracial blessing up for adoption despite Joanie's objection.

When her mother threatened this, Joanie vowed that, should her baby be taken away from her and put up for adoption, she would go back home and furiously fuck until she was seeded again and again gave birth. For the fine Mills family, it was a no-win situation. To lessen the blow to their family name, Mrs. Mills came up with a compromise.

She would allow Joanie to keep and raise her ebony baby under one condition. She insisted that Joanie reveal the name of the black boy who'd impregnated her and claim that he had raped her. Joanie decided to oblige. A lifetime with her baby was more valuable than the fifteen minutes it took to make him.

As it turned out, Joanie's suitor was Bryan Campton, a senior at her school. His family was one of the few clusters of black folk residing inward past Third Square. They'd moved to Second Square some time last year, shortly before he and Joanie enjoyed their romp, after Right Realty Company decided to let a few coloreds into the better neighborhoods for fear of facing an inevitable lawsuit under some relative of the Civil Rights, or Fair Housing, Act.

Many people, such as the sheriff, resented the negroid presence past Third Square. Many people, such as the sheriff, wanted to bleach the neighborhood and oust these black residents.

But now, there was a chance for something more. There was a chance to make them pay for their social crime, to make them pay for invading white territory and white vaginas. Bryan would be prosecuted for rape. And Margo would do her best to cleverly botch his trial.

Another deal had already been made with the District Attorney's Office—one to ensure that, though the matter was somewhat stale and there was no "evidence" other than Joanie's testimony and child, the DA would take the case to court. It was now the perfect opportunity to make a deal with Margo.

As the Camptons were not rich people and would surely be denied a second mortgage on their house if they decided to so fund their son's defense, Margo would be the Public Defender assigned to Bryan's case. And, as Public Defender, Margo could see to it that closet racists were selected during voir dire; that witnesses who could redeem Bryan's character, or hue Joanie as a whore, never made it to the stand; and, that her general defense efforts were somehow subdued, whether by less conspicuous means such as her demeanor or voice or by legal arguments that barely cut the mustard.

She could do all of this, of course, without putting her career on the line—for Margo was a very skilled attorney who could zealously represent her client without zeal. Her representation of her client would be competent and complete. She'd creatively forge the cracks through which justice could slip.

Granted, however, Margo could only pledge to do her worst in representing Bryan. Not even she could be certain that the jury would actually convict him. And, certainly, he would appeal an unfavorable verdict which probably would be overturned.

But, despite the deliberation and writs Margo could not control, the mere trial, the sheriff believed, would be enough to upset the Campton family. The Camptons would suffer the indignity and the disgrace of the trial irrespective of the verdict or appeal. Bryan would forever be labeled a "rapist" and a "miscreant nigger" regardless of any sooner or later acquittal. This, the sheriff hoped, would be enough to scare the Camptons out of Second Square, maybe out of this town, and to give the white folk even more reason to hate the blacks. This would allow the whites to win the human race in this town.

In exchange for her efforts, or lack thereof, Margo would get silence on the unfortunate matter that befell her, "People up 'n leave town without any reason or explanation. People just up 'n leave. Tell 'em she up 'n left. You'll be safe with that story, I guarantee. Aint nobody gonna wonder where she gone or why she aint said nothin' before she left. Damn, her whole family's dead, and she don't got too many friends other than that retard that don't talk. Who's gonna ask? Who's gonna care? You just tell 'em she gone away. I'll handle the dirty work for ya'. You just see to it that the nigger pays."

~ 17 ~

These negotiations took place two days after Tad left her and two days before Tad knocked on Margo's door. For two days, neither Margo nor David noticed that she wasn't around or alive.

Margo had gone to her room, likely to make sure it was in order or to check on the surplus supply of toilet tissue in her tiny bathroom, five hours prior to this meeting with the sheriff.

When Margo opened the bedroom door, she met a scene she couldn't have imagined. The first thing she noticed was the disarray of the room—the objects set out and flecked with notes. It took Margo a moment to see her body. But when she saw her body, there was no question that she was dead.

Her skin was mostly pale, so much more than ever usual, with lines of empty veins cracked over every inch of visible skin. Margo didn't need to touch her body to know that it was hard and dry. The naked parts of her body slowly darkened to rich lines of purple which rigidly rested on the surface of the bed. Rigamortis had set in long ago, and gravity had pulled the blood from her veins to the back of her body.

Margo shouted for David, "David! David, come quick!" When David arrived at the scene, Margo's body blocked his full view of the room so that he could see the mess but not the loss. His first inquiry was as to why the room was in such disorder. He gasped as Margo stepped aside to reveal the room's victim.

"She's obviously dead. She must have killed herself," David offered.

"Oh, David, you're such a genius! You really know how to read the clues."

"How long has she been like this? It looks like a while. I can't remember the last time I saw her."

"I don't know how long she's been dead! All that matters is that she is. We need to figure this out. We'll have to take care of this."

So started five hours of anxious discussion. Margo and David explored their options as they explored the room. They noticed the empty pill and vodka bottles. They read the notes and instructions. Eventually, they came to a conclusion.

They would keep her death, her suicide, a secret. None would be the wiser so that none could judge or chastise the barrister and her spouse. It was this pride that Margo and David had in common with the Millses—a common thread, though Margo didn't realize it at the time, with which she could weave a devious plot.

Margo went to see the sheriff that evening willing to pay whatever price he suggested. How perfectly appropriate his terms turned out to be.

After the deal had been haggled, Margo returned home, where she and David packed up all of the scattered belongings in the upstairs catacomb. They carried four large boxes of trinkets, notes, and decrees down to the alcove between their kitchen and backdoor.

A few hours later, when late night brimmed on early morning, the sheriff came and knocked on the door. He'd parked the paddy wagon behind their house, flushed close to the back porch.

The sheriff went upstairs and, with David's help, carried her body down the stairs as Margo loaded the paddy wagon with the boxes of her belongings. She was the last item tossed into the mix.

Margo stood by the door and watched as the sheriff and David each stepped into the front seats of the police vehicle before the sheriff drove off. She went back into the house to clean what mess remained.

Together, the sheriff and David traveled to the local Pet Society—the dog pound. It was closed at this late hour. But that didn't matter much since they weren't looking for a pet. The sheriff had a key which he used to open the delivery door. They hauled her body and her possessions, in turn, through the double doors and down a long corridor.

If her ears had still been able to hear, she would have heard dogs barking and yelping canine prayers for attention or canine cries of objection. She would have heard the roar of the incinerator when the sheriff turned the switch to spark its fire.

They put her, and the tangibles of her testament, in the same incinerator in which too many old animals, including Mollie, and unwanted litters had been put to ash and dust. They stood there as her skin crackled and withered under the blaze. The smell of burning human flesh mixed with the scent of musty pet urine and feces that still dangled in the air.

By the practice of the Pet Society, the incinerator had been set to burn for a specific amount of time equal to the time it takes to char and reduce the body of an average household pet. Because she, however, was no average household pet but a person, the sheriff had to flick the switch three times to ensure nothing of her form or frame remained intact. After three cycles, she and everything that was hers became but ash amongst other ash.

It was done. She was no more.

Neither David nor the sheriff thought to remove her ashes from the incinerator. Or, perhaps, they thought of it but couldn't be bothered with the task or plagued by its implications. It was sufficient to leave these cupfuls of her remains here. The staff would surely empty the incinerator's contents soon enough, long before their transgression would even be considered a possibility, should brows be raised.

If David had been more of a man, he might have scooped up her ashes to give her some type of proper ceremony. He could have sprinkled them over her family's graves or buried them in his backyard. Maybe said a prayer before flushing them down the toilet. The average household pet commonly got such treatment—shouldn't she?

Eh, again, she was no average household pet.

None of her requests had been fulfilled. Her belongings did not go to their designees, and she didn't get to wear her favorite suit one last time. No friends were called, no solemn authorities contacted. Instead, all things were put to fire—she, her possessions, and her desires. All things burnt, condensed to grey.

Margo, David, and the sheriff disposed of her so easily. In the following days, there were few inquiries as to her whereabouts. Indeed, Tad was the first to inquire—the first to be dished the fiction that she had left town and moved to Venice. A few others soon asked, each taking the tall tale at its face without challenging Margo's claim or soliciting further information.

She disappeared from this town, from this earth, without much attention from others. There was no true sadness, mourning, or loss. She hadn't passed. She'd merely passed through.

Her life was lived like water. She was something so fluid and dynamic. Sometimes calm, sometimes raging, she made herself abundantly available to others who simply took her for granted. She was taken in, consumed, allowed to nourish whatever thirsts one had, and then pissed away with little or no concern or appreciation.

No one read the label; none distilled the truth. They idly let her pass through their systems and trickle down into a greater one, flushed from here into oblivion. One drop in an ocean, a pool, a toilet, she was lost in something far larger than she—and those others never thought twice, for they'd already gotten what they needed and stood turgid.

Like water, so pure yet imperfect. Muddied, chemically treated, processed. *Lukewarm.*

When water met fire, she was the one extinguished.

~ 18 ~

I don't know if that's what actually happened. But it makes the most sense. It's the best explanation I can come up with.

I'm sorry. I know I've transgressed a grave literary boundary, broken some author's rule of thumb, in shifting from the third person to the first person at this point in the account. But I would've hoped you'd known all along that it was me telling this story.

I don't expect you to come to any type of astonishing revelation—to find some boy meets girl beauty or a silver lining. You can draw whatever romanticized conclusions you want.

Feel free to believe that I'm writing this because she gave me a voice. Feel free to believe that I'm writing this for her, to put her words on paper in order to keep a part of her alive forever and to have you know that she was real—or, believe that this is the eulogy, the farewell speech, she never got.

Believe what you will, but, please, don't be foolish.

I write this for myself.

For over a year, I've been trying to figure out what happened to her. Margo said she moved to Venice. But I was with her that night. I put those quarters on her eyes. I was there, for Christ's sake!

She was dead. Wasn't she? She'd swallowed those good pills and that cheap vodka. Hadn't she? She wasn't breathing. Was she?

What I saw had to be death. What I heard had to be a lie. It had to be. It had to be death and deception.

I can only speculate on how Margo and David made that

lie work. I never saw Margo talk to the sheriff. I never saw David and the sheriff take her to the pound and burn her. I wasn't there, so I don't know if it's true at all. But I tell myself it is—because I was there for everything else, everything that happened before and after she passed through.

Bryan did go to trial for "raping" Joanie. He was convicted. And now, he sits in some dank cell awaiting his appeal. The Camptons weren't pleased with Margo's counsel, though they couldn't find any errors egregious enough to warrant professional sanctions.

They decided to hire a big wig attorney from another town to represent Bryan in his appeal. Of course, they couldn't afford it. And since they couldn't get a second mortgage on their Second Square house, they had to sell it. They moved into an apartment back on Fifth Square, even farther removed from the town's heart than where they'd originally lived. They pray for a reversal of Bryan's conviction every day so that the whole family can move out of this town to somewhere where the threatening phone calls, the slashing of their tires, and the condescending whispers and glares will not be found.

Bryan faces time, and the "niggers" were ousted from Second Square, because Margo wasn't really on the ball at Bryan's trial. I saw parts of the trial and read about the rest in the papers, just like I'd seen and read about many other of Margo's clients and cases. She really could have done a better job in every facet of what she presented.

Margo wore black and white to court every day during Bryan's trial, black suits on white blouses. It seemed to me that this was a poor wardrobe selection. The greyscale was serious and stern, not to mention suggestive. This had to've stirred something in the jury—a subconscious reminder, or confirmation, of the fatal element of the essential crime of which Bryan was accused, black overpowering white.

Margo's interactions with Bryan were mechanical and distant. She never touched him, never got too close. She cowered in his presence, as if she were in the presence of none other than a rapist. This too had to've stirred something in the jury—if Bryan's lawyer was afraid of him, he must be guilty.

The jury itself was no lot of outstanding citizens. Bryan's "peers" were all white, mostly middle-aged parents with children, mostly daughters, in their mid-teen years. More than two of them where the offspring of others whose fathers once wore white sheets from head to toe and had a proclivity for burning crosses. With a jury like that, the verdict did not come as a surprise.

The jury's decision was swift, reached after only 45 minutes at the close of the barrister's brawl. Though, a "brawl" I would not necessarily call it. Margo's voice was weak throughout the trial. She spoke softly without much inflection or passion. She used a lot of technical jargon that I didn't really understand, and she was quick to her points.

Margo's performance, and Bryan's and the Camptons' fates, are what lead me to believe that Margo was operating under some incentive. Bryan's demise was so close to her death, her departure to Venice, that it seems too timely and canny to be chance alone.

I can't help but think the two are unfortunately related. I can't help but see Margo entwined in some back-scratching, and the sheriff is the one with the scaliest back. Two months ago, he himself was arrested, and now awaits trial, on charges of being an accessory, after the fact, to vehicular manslaughter; conspiracy to cover up a crime; bribery; attempted bribery; and, multiple charges for misuse of his police authority.

Dan Spetzl, an open-minded animal rights activist who gave up a rewarding career as an advertisement executive to pursue a humane nonprofit campaign, recently came to town after a tour of other regional cities where he preached the importance of public awareness as to the necessity of spaying and neutering pet dogs and cats.

Spetzl used his advertising knowledge to assess a city's or a town's commercial and entertainment interests and then developed public service announcements, postings, and pamphlets that somehow used those interests to effectively deliver his message to the local public.

Stan Jopps, the head vet and policy director at the Pet Society, was very pleased when Spetzl came to town. Indeed, this town had seen its fair share of excess and discarded litters, and Jopps was eager to have Spetzl help solve this problem.

Jopps and Spetzl had been fervently working on this project for nearly a week, often working straight through days and evenings into late night and early morning. They'd usually leave the pound before midnight, sometimes parting ways and other times going to Larry's for a side dish to their ala carte development.

They'd done just that one night—stayed at the pound until around midnight and then headed off to Larry's for food to feed their discussion. But, instead of going their separate ways at the end of the meal, they decided to go back to the pound so that Jopps could give Spetzl his files containing the statistics of peticides for the past five years, the before shot to what might come as the after to Spetzl's efforts.

When Spetzl and Jopps arrived back at the Pet Society, they discovered that they were not alone. They heard the incinerator blazing and found the sheriff, more than half past drunk, standing at its control.

Even though he was drunk, the sheriff refrained from acting too hastily. He could have pulled out his gun, shot them, and tossed them into the incinerator. But that would have been too messy. He'd have had to've cleaned up all that blood. And Jopps and Spetzl weren't persons whose absences would go unnoticed. Instead, he insisted he was there on "police business."

When Jopps wanted to know what kind of business, when he argued that no "police business" would require or permit the sheriff to be on the premises at this late hour without he or some other Pet Society staff knowing, the sheriff tried to bribe them, offering them money to turn and walk out of the room and to ask no questions or tell no others what they'd seen.

Both Jopps and Spetzl refused this offer, either out of morality, responsibility, or offense that the proffered sum was only $1,000 apiece. Again, the sheriff refrained from acting too hastily. Again, he could have pulled out his gun and shot them. He could have explained it away—perhaps saying they'd entered the pound unannounced to commit some malfeasance and that he shot them in the line of duty.

But, still yet, this would've been too messy. He'd have to come up with a story about their criminal attempts. He'd have to explain why he was there and why he was drunk and used excessive police force. He'd have to worry that someone might discover what he'd put in the incinerator.

It's a pity for him that he wasn't smart enough to consider that he could have used all of his concerns to his advantage—he could have shot them and told a fabulous fabrication. He could have covered up all of his own illegal acts by saying that he saw them commit a crime, followed them to the pound, and confronted them when they used the incinerator to burn the evidence.

He wasn't smart or sober enough to realize this though. The incinerator was nearing the end of its second cycle, and he hoped this would be enough. He had no other options, so he stood and waited while Spetzl called the sheriff's station and reported the incident on his cell phone.

To make sure that the sheriff's deputies wouldn't arrive at the scene to only find Spetzl and Jopps or to help the sheriff finish whatever he was doing, Spetzl made two other calls—one to the state police and another to the local television station.

The media, as usual, was the first to get there, followed by the sheriff's deputies ten minutes later and the state police before the end of the hour. The incinerator's second cycle was complete by this time. There hadn't been a third. The sheriff was hauled off by the state police as other state officers guarded the incinerator while it cooled down so that they could inspect it.

The state forensic team discovered a large hipbone in the incinerator. It was too large to be a common animal bone—too large to be that of even the largest hound or mastiff.

After a few hours, it was determined to be a human hipbone. The sheriff had remained silent and in state police custody for those few hours. When the trooper who'd been attempting to interrogate him was called out of the room and returned with a "you're screwed" grin on his face, the sheriff understood that two cycles hadn't been enough. The trooper confronted the sheriff with the facts, told him that a human hipbone had been discovered, and informed him that he would eventually be charged with murder when more facts, as surely they would be, unfolded.

Faced with a charge of murder, the sheriff decided to speak. He made his admission, "I didn't kill her. I just put her in there to get rid of the body."

"Who was she?"

"Alice. Alice Worth. Nothin' but an old cripple, used to be a whore."

"If you didn't kill her, who did?"

The sheriff's story unfolded as follows: He'd been out drinking with Paul Ridge, a generically local generic businessman, earlier that evening. They were both extremely drunk when they left the bar but drove their respective cars nonetheless. The sheriff was behind Ridge's car on a lonely street when Ridge slammed on his brakes and veered off of the road. Ridge'd hit something. The sheriff pulled over behind him.

That something turned out to be a someone—Alice Worth. She'd been crossing the street like a chicken, to get to the other side. She was bloodied and broken. Clearly dead.

Ridge was the one who hit her; he would've been the one to pay for this crime. But he decided to pay with money rather than time. Though the sheriff didn't admit this to the trooper at the time—it only came out after Ridge was apprehended and told his side of the story—the sheriff told Ridge he'd take care of the body for a payoff of five grand.

The sheriff took Alice's body to the pound and tossed it into the incinerator. He was to receive $5,000 cash the next morning. Obviously, he never got paid.

The news spread through town like wildfire and many wondered what other foul things the sheriff had done in the course of his career. I'm sure there were people who knew some of the sheriff's secrets—people who were involved or who had bartered with him. But those lips remained sealed. Even though no further indiscretions were disclosed, rumors crowded the streets about who else the sheriff might have burned.

Yet, no one ever mentioned her.

I'm the one who's mentioning her now. I'm the one who wonders if the sheriff put her in the incinerator just like he'd done with Alice.

Had she ended up like Alice after all?

It makes sense. All the pieces fall into place. The death no one knows I saw, the suicide I witnessed, was something Margo wanted to get rid of. The sheriff is a racist and wanted the Camptons out of Second Square. They each got what they wanted, didn't they?

Do you see the link? I do.

I do, because I want to.

I was there that night, damn it. I saw her with my own two eyes. I know what happened.

But Margo told me otherwise. Margo told me she left, that she moved to Venice. I did not see her move to Venice. I saw her die. If I can't trust what I see with my own eyes, what else is there?

My truth and reality have been called into question. I doubt myself and everything I ever thought I knew.

~ 19 ~

I'll do it. I'll press the button.

REWIND. Back to that night.

I am in your room.

I'm sitting there in the maroon velvet chair, leaning forward over my sprawled legs with my elbows resting inches above my knees. My posture is as tight and rigid as the panic and anxiety that bolt against my nerves.

I eye the wonders of your room, frightened by how it has been enlivened. Hidden things have found their ways to the surface; buried pieces have been unearthed.

The room isn't dirty. It's just messy, clattered with clusters of your custody. There's something unsettling about this display. Something gruesome and something absurd.

I see your favorite black polyester suit and purple satin blouse carefully folded and placed atop the bench at the bed's foot. Your jewelry case. Your black sandals.

The roller-top desk behind me is open. It brims with discrete licks of piled books, full little boxes, and filled paper bags.

There're things laid out all over your dresser as well. Some folded things. Probably scarves or handkerchiefs. A set of four shot glasses in the shape of tiny guitars. One is chipped. You, the broken one in a set of four.

A clear- and blue- glass penguin figurine. A cherry-wood trinket box. More books, boxes, and bags. Everything is covered with Post-it® notes.

These things are not meant to bleed grace—they are your will, your last will and testament.

There's a note on your nightstand, on top of that blood leather-bound spiral notebook in which you regularly scribble down appointments, contact information, and residual thoughts.

I'll read the note before I leave.

You're lying on the bed. You are wearing a pants and top set of faded crimson red. Your long waves of hair are pulled to a tight ponytail at the back of your head.

Is this a special occasion? Do you want, need, to feel pretty?

You're limp and at haft-mast on the tautly made bed.

Your hair is subtly darker than usual. It looks damp but very clean. You must have just bathed. Your skin looks rosier than its norm. It's reflecting, refracting, or absorbing the red fabric that covers most of your body.

You look like a larger-than-life ragdoll carefully positioned on a showroom bed. You're propped up by pillows, your arms at your sides. Your palms are up, and your fingers are curled. You are waiting to catch Jesus's, or God's, precipitous reignfall.

Your legs are extended outward from the apex of your sex, gradually widening to your duck-pointed bare feet.

In the gape of your legs, near your knees and at a logical toss-point from your left hand, I see it. An empty fifth of Vladimir™ Vodka.

You tell me you took good pills and drank vodka.

I hadn't immediately noticed the small tan prescription pill bottle at the side of your right hip. But I see it now. The lid is off and the bottle is empty.

Wait!

I didn't see you take the pills. I didn't see you drink the vodka. All I see are empty bottles. How much of either, how much of both, did you consume? I have no idea.

I can't stand to look at you as you speak. You try to hold your head up to look at me. It keeps falling back above the pillows. The pills and the vodka are working tragically magic spells on your body. Your neurons are being seduced. Your sarcomeres are being raped.

Your neck and head are the only parts of your body that are moving. The rest of you is fixed in position.

The words you speak are affronted and slow, lost in each other and far from crisp. You speak at a slur, with relaxed nasal "nnn" noises swimming the suspensions of your speech.

You make a barely audible startled gasp, consisting of a trinity of rapid inhalations in heightening volume and speed, each time your head unwillingly drops back.

When you trigger your head forward again, you quickly and loudly exhale as if you've either found some sense of relief or just ran an exhaustingly big race.

But what is this? Is this the early stage of a death or the late stage of a drunken stupor?

Is this death I am watching?

You drink a lot, always have. You take pills for fun, always have. You do both together, always have. What is this? Is this like always, or is it something different?

I've seen dead before, but never dying. Never seen fleeing, escaping.

How many pills? How many shots of vodka? How much would it take for you to kill you? Was it that you never took enough of either before? Did you take enough of each tonight?

You are apologizing to me, telling me it's not my fault. I don't know what you're talking about. Nothing of this is my fault.

You tell me I didn't kill anyone, and that I didn't kill him.

It hits me like a sonic boom, a tidal wave, and many other

bad clichés. I know of what you speak.

Ancient demons are awakened, extinguished memories burst once again into flames—I remember. I see you and him together.

You're both in his office. You are bent over his desk. He's behind you.

The snake. The forbidden fruit.

You are both naked, the man and you, the woman that isn't his wife, and are not ashamed. Not even as you fuck.

I hear him utter God's name. Misplaced prayer—God can't hear either one of you right now. He stopped listening to you, he cast you out, when you were beguiled by the serpent and you both did succumb.

I wake from the daze of memories that had just been roused in me. But I'm still lost in my own thoughts.

Tell me, was this what you meant when you spoke of sin? Is this that thing of which I washed you clean?

This is what you wanted me to forgive you for—why you asked me, of all people, to baptize you.

My head is spinning.

I never thought that I killed him. I never felt any guilt over his death. Never any responsibility. I was just a kid who told a secret about something I'd seen.

I heard your voices in the office and saw that you both were naked, and then I knew shame. Shame that humbled me against the faults of my own gender. Shame that silenced me, leaving me to watch what I say because I once said what I watched.

Surely your God must have felt shame too. Shame for the faults of a being he created in his own image. And shame that he had weaknesses too—that he simply couldn't turn and look the other way. Like me, in my likeness, he saw. Like me, in my likeness, your God reacted.

I lost the memories but kept the shame. And now, they've both met each other again.

Is this an explanation?

I jump up to speak, "This guilt? It was never mine. It belonged only to you."

As soon as I say these words, I realize it is too late. It is done.

Or is it?

I fall back into the oversized chair. I look to the ceiling, then to the floor. I am looking for your soul. If it escaped, I don't see it.

I stand up again. I look around the room. It's so bright in here. It's dimly lit but still so bright. It must be the colors. I feel woozy. I am wavering. I almost fall forward. No, I catch myself.

My mind is flooding. I see you and him. I hear you. What is this? Then or now? Am I in the past or the present?

I see things that never happened. It's all mixed up together.

The chunks of broken glass.

The puddle of lukewarm water.

The bottle of vodka. The little yellow notes.

Flowing, flowing—past and present. Resonance. nnn's. a's. m's. f's. h's. Dissonance. Doped-up and dancing. The chocolate syrup. The prescription pills. Where is the lid? Hair, swaying. Hair, damp and darkened.

Two deaths—none little, none real?

I didn't do it. It's not my fault. But I'll do it now.

I feel my temperature rising. I'm so hot that everything around me feels cool, cooler, and cold. It feels like my head is empty. I can't understand this. I can't think straight.

I wonder what a real man would do.

I walk to the foot of the bed and slowly round its lower right corner. I stare down at your wilted visage. My left hand grazes your left foot. It's soft and full. It's still so warm.

What would the Good Reverend do?

I see you and him together again. I picture you in carnal embrace. I want to have you—like he did. Pity, I never had my turn.

What about John Wayne?

I glide to the head of the bed. I kneel down on the floor and perch my hands on the edge of the mattress. I kneel here neither to pray nor to be the Romeo to your miscast Juliet but to pollute my mind with new memories to couple with shame.

What would your own father do?

I won't sing for you. I'm not your prince. It's someday, yet I haven't come. I haven't cum. But I want to. For you, I want to. I want you.

I am ashamed to want you. You are lifeless on this bed, but I still want you. I could have you, and no one would know.

I disgust myself.

I stare at you as if time has stopped. I study every inch of you. I sip the air around you. I feel dizzy, woozy again.

I am so ashamed of what I feel. This shame overcomes me. I cannot, I will not, do what I want to do. I can bring you no redemption. I cannot flush you with life's glow.

I cannot have you.

I will not be a man at your bed. I will not take what was not offered.

Oh, how I disgust myself! I am gruesome. I am absurd.

I can stand to be here no longer. I'm so damn tired—I need a break from all this shit.

I want to leave. Still dizzy, I rise to my feet. I stare down at your face. You have eyes like quarters. I reach my right hand into the front right pocket of my jeans, scraping my swollen self, and pull out two quarters—one for each of your eyes.

Big eyes, covered with quarters, closed forever.

I read the note. I turn. I leave.

~ 20 ~

And so went the Seventh Day.

Those were the audios and visuals that affronted my senses. Those were the thoughts and deliberations that assaulted my mind. But who's to say what really happened that night—or what happened after I left?

It's entirely possible that she didn't consume the pills and alcohol in a deadly enough combination. Perhaps she'd merely passed out from the pills and booze, breathing quick shallow breaths my own heat and confusion would allow me neither to hear nor to see. She could've woken up, both from the spell of the intoxicants and from whatever other daze she'd been in, and packed up her stuff and blew town without turning back.

Or, maybe Margo or David found her there with a couple breaths left in her and called for some inconspicuous homecare to bring her out of her trance. Maybe they saved her life and then forced her off to Venice for holiday or life, or to a near or distant psychiatric asylum under a false name.

Possibly, she never really intended to take her life. Maybe she was playing a cruel, or merciful, joke, and I was the punch line. Maybe, all along, she'd intended to leave town but didn't know how to tell me. Maybe, all along, she'd thought, like the rest of them, I was a retard who wouldn't understand why she wanted to leave and would try to make her stay or to go with her. So, maybe, she set up this elaborate farce to pull a trick on me.

Or, maybe something else transpired when I walked out of the room. Maybe something else died. Perhaps, despite her careful thought on the matter, she had, in action, chosen the wrong means to bring about her demise. It could be that what she got was not what she wanted.

She'd fancied her mind the manifestation of her soul and she, thinking as her soul, wanted to escape her body. She'd claim it was her soul that acted. It acted to escape. But maybe it didn't. Maybe her soul ended up releasing her body.

Probably by some miscalculation or by the sympathy, empathy, or pain it felt watching her body die, maybe her soul felt bad for her body and set it free. This would be the catastrophic event she never talked about, the event which defied nature as she defined it—the death of her soul for the life of her body, a backwards altruism she could never comprehend.

Set free, released from a soul that wanted to die, maybe her body was still alive, or reborn, after I left. Maybe she jumped up, minutes or hours later, possibly the next day, and was nothing more than her body. With her crying soul dead, her body was free to move on—to Venice, perhaps?

Or, if she did die, in soul, body, or both, it could be that her body just vanished into thin air, disappeared, or was erased from the surface of the earth. Maybe God himself came down to carry her away, or Mother Earth opened wide and swallowed.

They say that the eyes are the windows to the soul. Maybe her soul couldn't climb out of either of its windows after I put those damn quarters on her eyes, and it got so frustrated and worked so hard until her body just imploded.

Could be a lot of different things that happened. The point is: I don't know.

I may never know. But it's better that way.

When a child is kidnapped or a loved one disappears, when someone is missing without a trace, their friends and families almost always confide that they'd want to know the whereabouts of their loved one, even if it meant finding out that their loved one was dead. Those friends and families believe that it's better to know the truth, how ever horrid it may be, than to wonder and know nothing.

Not me though. I don't feel that way. I'd rather not know what really happened. I do not seek the answer. I'm not after closure.

Anything I would find out for certain would be some fact I don't want or need to know. On the one hand, if I found out that what I saw that night and believed to be true was, in fact, true, it would mean she is dead. Gone. Done. It would mean she killed herself, that there was nothing in this world, not even me, that could sustain her.

On the other hand, if I found out she hadn't expired to full bodily death, that'd open a whole other can of worms. It could mean that she left this town without telling me, whether because that part of her that cared for me was dead or because it had never actually existed. It could mean that she was locked up somewhere, more of a captive than she'd ever been, giving her words to someone else or to no one at all.

I am not willing to accept either hand on its own. I do not like the exclusivity of any one conclusion. If the options remain open, I alone can bring her to life or to death as I alone see fit. It's my greatest joy to exercise this power.

Sometimes, I like to picture her riding on a gondola in a canal in Venice. She's smiling as the sun beams over her form. She's laughing, strands of her long hair blowing over her face. A pint of peach gelato melts beside her.

Other times, I picture her somewhere else. I picture her in heaven. With her family. Smiling and loving. Her worries and pains, relieved. She knows who killed Kurt Cobain. She knows many of God's secrets. And she's waiting for me.

What I want is for her to have everything, the pleasures

she'd enjoy in life and the comforts she'd find in death. She can have both in my mind, so long as I remain unaware of what really happened.

My ignorance is her bliss.